WHEN THE
NIGHT COMES

FAVEL PARRETT

SCEPTRE

First published in Great Britain in 2014 by Sceptre
An imprint of Hodder & Stoughton
An Hachette UK company

First published in paperback in 2015

1

A CIP catalogue record for this title is
available from the British Library

Paperback ISBN 978 1 848 54856 5
eBook ISBN 978 1 848 54855 8

Printed and bound by Clays Ltd, St Ives plc

Hodder & Stoughton policy is to use papers that are natural, renewable
and recyclable products and made from wood grown in sustainable
forests. The logging and manufacturing processes are expected to
conform to the environmental regulations of the country of origin.

Hodder & Stoughton Ltd
Carmelite House
50 Victoria Embankment
London EC4Y 0DZ

www.sceptrebooks.co.uk

Praise for *Past the Shallows*

'that rare thing, a finely crafted literary novel that is genuinely moving and full of heart' *The Age*

'Wintonesque' *Herald Sun*

'a wonderful story told with a voice that I wanted to listen to. A voice that will stay with me for a long time.'
Sydney Morning Herald

'a fresh and vital voice in Australian fiction'
The Australian Women's Weekly

'Parrett's writing is exquisite in its simplicity and eloquence, and her narrative is heart-rending. This poignant story resonates.' *Kirkus Reviews*

'An amazing book by a wonderful writer – Cormac McCarthy meets David Vann meets Favel Parrett. Read this book.'
Sunday Times

'clearly the work of a talented new novelist' *Weekend Australian*

'Parrett's debut marks the addition of a strong voice to the chorus of Australian literature.' *Canberra Times*

'her prose is as powerful as a rip' *The Australian*

'So real, so true – this novel sweeps you away in its tide.'
Robert Drewe

'Parrett's crystalline prose and her rhythmic sentences give the narrative a wave-like power.' *Australian Book Review*

Favel Parrett was the recipient of an Australian Society of Authors Mentorship in 2009 and has had a number of short stories published in various journals. *Past the Shallows*, her first published novel, was shortlisted for the 2012 Miles Franklin Award and won the Australian Book Industry's Newcomer of the Year Award Prize. Most recently she was awarded the Antarctic Arts Fellowship allowing her to travel to Antarctica to complete research for *When The Night Comes*. She balances her writing around surfing, travelling and volunteering at an animal shelter. She lives in Victoria, Australia with her partner and two dogs. You can find out more about Favel and her writing via her website www.favelparrett.com.au, or at www.hodder.co.uk. You can follow her on Twitter at www.twitter.com/favelparrett or find her on Facebook.

For my brother

For my brother

Blue white ice that floats on a moving sea
It is the opposite of grey
It is the opposite of everything I had known

Blue white ice that floats on a moving sky
It is the opposite of grey
It is the opposite of everything I had known

There was a time when Vikings filled our house and there were people and parties and Mum was happy then.

They were real Vikings. Big hulking Vikings who came from far away on a bright red ship, which busted through pack ice and made it all the way down to Antarctica. They had names like Anders and Bo and Finn and Henrik and they were all tall and blond, except for Bo, who had dark brown hair and grey-blue eyes. He was from a small island that was *the sunniest place in all of Denmark.*

Bo liked to walk and keep on walking. He liked the smell of wet grass. He made us pancakes with jam and cream and he could get a tiny bird to eat right out of the palm of his hand without even trying. When we went out for pizza he always ate two slices at once, one piece on top of the other with the toppings on the inside, like a pizza sandwich. He could eat four pieces to my one and I liked him very much.

Sometimes we would visit his ship. *Nella Dan* was all wood and brass and there were paintings in the mess – bright flowers and birds, green and orange and yellow. I liked to walk down the long passageways, go up all her stairs, from the bottom right up to the monkey deck and down again. I never grew tired of that.

I would pretend she was my home, that my cabin was down below, cosy and wood-lined with a bunk just for me. A warm snug doona and soft pillow, a round porthole that let the light in. All I needed.

It was never dark – it was never night.

Sleep now
Close your eyes, hold them tight
It's just a strange dream that comes in the darkness
Just a strange dream that comes in the night
Don't listen to the shouting
Don't listen for the sounds
It's just a strange dream that comes in the night-time
You are asleep

I am asleep.

Sleep now
Close your eyes, hold them tight
It's just a strange dream that comes in the darkness
Just a strange dream that comes in the night.
Don't listen to the shouting
Don't listen for the sounds
It's just a strange dream that comes in the night-time
You are asleep

I am asleep.

TO THE ISLAND

We had dinner in the canteen, at a wooden table and the chairs didn't move. They were stuck to the floor somehow.

Mum was quiet, and my brother was quiet, and when we finished eating a man in a white uniform came over and said that the ship was going through the heads soon and that the forecast was for very rough seas. He was only looking at Mum when he spoke. He told her that it was advisable to get the children to bed as soon as possible.

My brother fell asleep quickly, his small body tucked in tight on the top bunk. But I lay awake, waiting for the rough seas. Waiting to see what they would feel like so far down. Flights and flights of stairs down from the canteen and from the windows that looked out to the sky. Down where we were, there were no windows. Down where we were, there were only fluoro lights and bunk beds. The bathroom was down the passage and Mum had left us. She was upstairs somewhere, upstairs above us where there was air and I wished that she would come back.

I must have fallen asleep because when I woke the whole world was rocking and shaking and I was rolling in my bed. Not just from side to side, but up and down as well. Mum's bed was still made. She wasn't there.

When I tried to get out of bed, I fell over and was sick on the floor. My brother was looking at me, his hands stuck fast around the railings of the bunk bed, his face white like death.

'Where's Mum?' he asked, but I didn't know.

He got down somehow, down from the bunk, and he didn't fall. He stood holding on to the bed as the room turned over and over and he got a towel off Mum's bed and put it over the vomit on the floor. He helped me up and in our pyjamas we made it out the door and into the hall. Together we fell against the walls as the ship lunged, and we slowly moved towards the stairs. Up and up, gripping the rail. Up to the deck where the canteen was.

There was hardly anyone around, only a few people sitting in the carpeted lounge, sitting with their heads in their hands. The canteen was empty and I couldn't tell what time it was. Outside the windows it was dark.

Outside it was black.

Mum was sitting by herself on a bench attached to the wall of the ship under a perspex roof. We sat next to her, holding on to the bottom of the bench tightly.

Mum said that she would just have one more cigarette and then we could go inside. I looked at her white face and her white hands. She was always sitting places by herself

in the night – always sitting by herself having one more cigarette.

I told her that I had been sick and she wiped my forehead and cheek and said, 'I'm sorry. I'm so sorry.' It looked like she was crying. She said it was just the sea spray and the cold. And it was cold. It was freezing and windy, and the wind cut into your back like you had no skin at all. I could hear the water crack against the ship, feel it hit then hear the spray shoot up. Only I couldn't see it. I couldn't see anything past the light cast out on the deck.

Out there the world was raging in the blackness.

We were going to a new place.

We were sailing towards it in the night.

An island in the middle of the sea.

An island that was made of stone.

It was only the ship that was keeping us safe. Only thin layers of steel and an engine pumping away in the dark were keeping us above the water, which would gladly swallow us all up like we had never ever been.

MRS WILSON'S B & B

We stayed in a B & B.

It was where we lived when we first arrived, after we got off the ferry and off the bus that drove through flat farming land and towns made of stones and old red bricks. Mum used the payphone at the bus terminal in Hobart. She rang a place that was advertised on the information board and made a reservation. Abbey House Bed and Breakfast.

I don't think it was very far away but we had two big suitcases and my brother was tired, so we all got into a taxi that was waiting out the front of the bus station.

The taxi driver was a very big man. He was wearing a clean blue shirt and his buttons looked like they might pop open around his belly. He asked if it was our first time to 'The Island' and my brother said *yes,* but my mum said *no.* I sat in the back seat and tried to imagine Mum being here before, maybe with Dad or maybe when she was young with her parents, but I couldn't see it. I didn't know this place.

We weren't in the taxi for long. We went up a steep hill and then around some curved streets and we were there. Battery Point. There were old houses, wooden houses, bare stone houses on the narrow streets, but they all seemed empty, deserted and nothing moved. The sky was grey.

We stopped on a corner by a sign that said *Mona Street*.

'You will be able to walk to the market from here come Saturday,' the taxi driver said. He got out of the car and helped Mum with our suitcases.

Mrs Wilson owned the B & B. She made my brother and me a cooked breakfast every morning and we ate it at the breakfast bar that looked out to the rose garden – a cottage garden. It was a cottage, the B & B, an old wooden cottage with a white picket fence and everything. It was just about the nicest place I had ever lived, except that we didn't really live there. We were just staying there.

I liked staying there.

We stayed in a guestroom for a week and then we moved to a room at the back of the house that Mrs Wilson let us have for free. She told my mum that it was just until we got on our feet, until we got settled. I didn't know what that really meant. Mrs Wilson still wanted to make my brother and me a cooked breakfast every morning, but Mum said we should just have cereal and be polite.

Mum found a house to rent three doors down on the same street about two weeks later. It was maybe the worst house

in Battery Point. There were no other houses like it – dark and faded, set back in the shadows of the tall grand houses around it. Mum had to let out a room to afford the rent. The front room. The only nice room. My brother and I shared the attic, which had a slanting roof. It was okay except the wallpaper was peeling in parts near the ceiling and the only toilet was in the back garden. I didn't like going down there in the dark, or even in the day much. But the garden had a huge walnut tree that our attic window looked out on, and when the walnuts were ripe my brother and I would stuff ourselves, eat them until our mouths were itchy and we could eat no more. Then we would smash fallen walnuts open and scatter them around the garden for the birds, for the forest ravens that were waiting in the tree.

But I missed the B & B, how warm it was there, how bright. And sometimes after school, when my brother and I walked home from the ferry, Mrs Wilson would be at her gate, and she'd call us in, tea and cakes waiting.

RUN, RUN – KELLY'S STEPS

The cold made it hard to breathe, burnt my chest – the stone and the concrete hard under my frozen feet.

I'd take my brother's sleeve and pull him along the empty streets of Battery Point. Early, we'd walk quickly. Everything still like always – only us. Frost on the windows of parked cars, thick and opaque and stuck fast.

Mona Street, Francis Street, Hampden Road. At the end of Kelly Street there were steps down into darkness, the back of Salamanca all crumbled and decayed. Cuts in the quarry stone rounded, worn. A stone fortress, a gateway we had to pass.

Run, run – Kelly's steps.

Some of the steps were bowed and stained, and the stains looked like old blood rusted orange with time. Blood soaked into the stone. We'd go down one step at a time as quickly as we could. Down, down, and we'd try not to look ahead into the dark lane. But at the bottom, in the cold cobbled shadows, ghosts would claw at our

clothes, try to grab hold of our hair, whisper in the echo of the stone.

Can you help me?

Can you see me?

Don't leave me here.

I'd pull my brother's hand hard, and we'd run and run, not even breathe, until we were through. Until we were on the other side.

Light.

The open sky.

An avenue of elm trees, the wharf beyond.

We'd slow down, catch our breath, walk out across Salamanca Place. Out along the grass and under the trees, across the road to the long wooden jetty where we'd stand and wait for the ferry to come. We'd hardly talk. We'd just wait.

We'd try not to think about Kelly's steps, about how the dead pressed up against our skin in that dark place.

8

THERE WAS A MAN

The rain came down.

I had my japara on, the hood covering my head and my hands tucked up inside. It was too big for me, the japara, but still the heavy black material kept most of the rain out. My brother was sick, at home. He'd been coughing in the night and was probably on the couch under his doona watching TV, waiting for Mum to get up. It was really cold in that old house in Battery Point and there was no heater.

I didn't want to go to school. I thought about going home to look after my brother, but I didn't. I just kept standing there in the rain, waiting for the ferry.

It must have been really early – there was no one else at the jetty. I could see the air when I breathed and everything was water. I looked down, watched the rain fall on the slick, black surface of the river. The drops formed perfect circles that got bigger and bigger until I could no longer follow the whole circle at once. Time and space, the raindrops were separate. They fell in a kind of silence, but then the rain got

harder, suddenly bursting, and there were too many drops to follow. The whole surface of the water prickled up and became rough and jumbled. The stillness gone.

The rain smacked my japara hard and it sounded like being inside a tent. I turned so that the rain couldn't hit my face. I looked down at my feet, at my wet sneakers. I closed my eyes and listened to the rain, listened to it fall on my hood. I imagined that the ferry was coming, that it was heading this way, pushing the water forward, pushing in against the wooden jetty. When I opened my eyes the ferry would be here and the captain, Peter, would run down from the wheelhouse to throw the thick rope around the wooden pylon and then he would help us on, one by one.

I would go inside and get dry. I could get warm.

I counted twenty drops of rain on my hood, then another twenty, and another. I kept my eyes closed. I counted forty more for good luck, then I opened my eyes.

RED. Nothing but red. A bright red wall of steel.

A ship, as tall as a building, as big as the sky, and when I looked up there was a man standing against the rail.

He was tall, dressed in white, and he was waving. I turned around, but there was no one there behind me. There was only me. Me, standing on the little jetty opposite this giant ship, the hood of my japara covering half my face and I knew the man couldn't see my eyes, my hair. He waved again like he knew me. He waved.

Someone could see me.

I waved back, my hand still tucked up in my japara sleeve. We were both standing in the rain, the black water between us, and I don't know why he was waving, but I waved back. I took notice.

A red ship. A red flag flying in the breeze. A man dressed in white.

Then a horn blew and I nearly jumped out of my skin. It was the ferry. People came from out of the grey nothing behind me, men in suits, other kids who caught the ferry to school, but everything was dull compared to the red. They were like fog, these people, blended into the grey rain and the concrete.

When I looked back up at the ship, the man was gone. A patch of sunlight broke through the clouds, hit the red bow, just a tiny beam. For a second there was nothing else but the words written clear, white against red: *Nella Dan*.

I said the words over and over in my head.

Nella Dan.

Nella Dan.

Nella Dan.

They made my heart beat out faster.

MS *Nella Dan*
Voyage 1, 1986/1987 Season
15th September 1986
Position: 46° 45.000' S, 147° 27.000' E
Captain's note: Objectives of this voyage are to complete the survey of Heard Island, and undertake the Antarctic Division BIOMASS Experiment – ADBEX III (survey krill and other zooplankton).

We have made good progress, however we have remained in a southerly direction all night in order to minimise the effect of the severe weather system.

I wake – my eyes wide.

Water smashes in against the port side and we swing wild. I cling to my bunk, my fingers grip the sheets, but my body rolls so far over that I end up against the bulkhead.

I rest there. I lie right up on that thin wall, my duvet entwined around my feet.

Come up, Nella. Right up.

I lie still. I wait.

Come up.

She does.

I fall back onto my bunk, take a deep breath. I keep breathing, strain to listen.

The water hits hard again and we pitch over. I tense my core but I'm back against the bulkhead, sliding up towards the ceiling. I feel *Nella* shudder, grind her metal teeth. My bones vibrate against her. I try to relax, keep calm – *it's fine* – but there's this creaking, this screeching, like every bolt that holds her together is coming loose. Coming apart.

Come up, Nella. Right up.

I feel her strain.

We snap back with a jolt and my duvet flings across the cabin. I think about getting off my bunk to get it, but it is not cold. *I'm* not cold. I don't know how long we have been in this storm. I was somewhere else, dead, not even dreaming.

Now I am here, in a cabin on a ship.

Now I am here, the Southern Ocean.

I reach for my clock, but it's not under my pillow. I feel *Nella* try to pull in, face the swell. Her energy races through me.

Come on, Nella – ride straight!

My cabin door flies open and light pours through. A silhouette staggers in, arms outstretched.

'Hey, Bo,' it says.

It's Soren.

'What time is it?' I yell.

He doesn't answer, but I can see him now – his face, his hair all messed up. I touch my own hair, feel how it's standing up at the back from sliding around my bunk.

We go over again, pitch sharp. The fastenings on the curtains bust loose and let in this strange light. I'm looking down from my bunk into green and blue. Looking down into water right there through my porthole. My cabin underwater – cold and deep.

'Christ,' Soren says as he slides down to the floor. He's wearing his big jacket like he's thinking of going outside, like he's thinking about going out for a walk or something. He has a bottle in his hand.

'Cheers!' he says loudly, and he leans up, swigs from the bottle. *Nella* comes back hard and everything's the right way for a moment. I take advantage of the gravity, roll off the bunk. I find my trousers, my jumper, put them on quickly.

A boot flings across the room, hits my leg. Something rolls around the floor – something hard. My travel clock. I grab it, shove it under my mattress. Coathangers bang around inside the cupboard and we go over again. I brace against the bunk.

Soren starts to laugh like a maniac. I think maybe he's drunk. I try to help him to his feet but it's hard to stand, hard to do anything. I let go of him. I drop to my knees, put my hands on the floor and I start to laugh too. I give in.

We make it out to the hall. We slide down the bulkhead and sit on the floor under the bright fluoro light. Soren winks at me, hands me the bottle. Whisky. Canadian Club.

'It's my birthday,' he says.

I look at him, at his face. I can't tell if he's joking.

'Happy birthday,' I say.

I wait for *Nella* to steady, put the bottle to my lips. I take a big gulp. It burns like crazy but soon I get the warmth, the glow. It creeps up my neck and face.

'It's really my birthday tomorrow,' he says, 'but no sleep, so I say it's my birthday now!' He puts his hand up in the air, pumps his fist. Victory.

We pitch down.

I slide backwards up the bulkhead, spin away from him along the passage. I nearly spill the whisky. I hear glass smash upstairs, furniture scrape and move. The cargo – God, the cargo stretching the chains, trying to break free one millimetre at a time. Did I secure everything right in the galley last night? I can't remember. The fridges, the freezers, all the things that could become mush. Tomatoes, melons, all those eggs.

I look down at my feet. I'm just wearing socks. One is blue and one is black. Close enough, I guess. I think about going up to check the galley, but there is nothing I can do really. Not now.

None of it matters.

We come back to the floor. Soren takes the bottle from my hands.

'Let's just sit here,' he says, like we were on the way somewhere else.

I look at him, his face all shiny with alcohol. I don't know why he didn't tell me it was his birthday. I don't know why he didn't say. I wonder if I have anything that I can give him.

'Okay,' I say. 'Let's just sit here.'

Away from portholes underwater, away from flying objects not secured. Let's just sit here down low, in the middle of our ship. Let's stay here.

Soren passes me the bottle again. I take a deep drink. I have catching up to do.

The chain for the fire hose swings out, reaches for the opposite bulkhead. I watch it swing, watch it touch the bulkhead and scrape up against it. Sometimes the chain coils down when we go over for a long time, sometimes it snakes right down – a foot or more of chain resting there on the wall. I can't take my eyes from it, the movement. This strange sideways gravity.

From the rub marks on the bulkhead, I know that *Nella* has pitched much further than this. Much further. We are safe. The chain becomes our barometer, our comfort. The chain becomes our drinking game. When the chain rests on the bulkhead for more than five seconds we drink.

We watch it swing.

We count.

We cheer.

The warmth is all through me now. I'm in this bubble of warmth, of light. I'm in this bubble.

Soren points at me, at my face. 'You have to come in with me,' he says. He pokes my shoulder hard. 'We'll do food, bar food. Our music on the stereo. Our place!'

He's talking about his bar again. The one he always talks about. The one he is going to start in the meat-packing district of Copenhagen.

People will come, you wait! Someone will turn all those warehouses into apartments. Students, couples, young people. They will all need a place to drink – I tell you!

He's pointing at me again. I can't help but smile. I think about people living in the old slaughterhouses, cold and open and draughty, all bent with time and age. I can't see it, but his enthusiasm is infectious.

'Deal?' he says.

'Okay,' I say, 'deal.'

We shake hands. His eyes only half-open now, not really focusing on anything. He's twenty-one.

I think how young that is. I think of all that is to come for him. I feel so happy for him, so excited for his time ahead. Time belongs to him.

'Happy birthday,' I say again. I take the bottle and look at him, look in his eyes. 'Skål,' I say. We are together. Comrades. Brothers-in-arms.

The chain swings.

The air conditioning is churning round the smell of aftershave. Someone's bottle must have smashed, one of the expeditioners, and the smell fills the lower decks, fills our passageway. It fills my lungs.

Soren takes a mouthful of whisky, but it comes spitting out, with laughter. With disgust.

'God, aftershave really stinks,' he says. He wipes his mouth. 'You have to make me a cake,' he hiccups.

One of my eyes is twitching now. I hold my eyelid down with my fingers. He pokes my shoulder.

'A cake,' he says again.

'What kind?' I ask.

'Ice-cream,' he says after forever. After thinking hard.

Out of all the cakes, he chooses something impossible. I think about the ingredients. I think about all the cakes I have made in my life. I can make any kind of cake but I've never made an ice-cream cake.

My father used to send me a birthday cake every year. Every year, even though he was so far away, always at sea. Once it was an ice-cream cake with a penguin on it.

A radioman. He could organise these things.

'I only ever spent five birthdays with my father,' I say, suddenly, out loud. I hold out my hand. Four fingers and a thumb. I look at them. They tingle, my fingers. The edges are blurry.

Soren looks at me.

'My father wasn't a sailor,' he says and he takes a gulp. 'Pigs,' he says, and he bursts out laughing.

I can hardly breathe I'm laughing so hard. I hear him say 'pigs' again in a high-pitched voice, almost a squeal that can't quite get out. We laugh together until there is nothing left.

Nella pitches, we go up the bulkhead. Soren slides on his side and I lie on my back. The chain rests down, but neither of us can drink anymore.

And maybe it's the talk of pigs, or the whisky, but I'm suddenly hungry. Starving. I look at Soren. I can't imagine him as a farmer. I can't imagine him surrounded by pigs, and grass and wide-open land. But I can see him in his bar with all that industrial mess and chaos and music. I can see that. His dream is good.

We make it up the steep stairs, pass Jens the chief engineer on the way. He nods at us, grease on his hands, on his jumpsuit. He looks done in. I go to ask him if he needs anything, but he waves me off, keeps on walking. I had almost forgotten that there were people up and working – up on the bridge and down in the engine room, the night crew keeping the rest of us safe. Keeping us going in the night, keeping watch in the storm. Heading south.

The galley is in okay shape, knives and pans secure. A few plates smashed, a few cups. A thermos on the floor, rolling around. I pick it up, secure it in its spot.

Klaus locks up the store cupboards to keep out the hungry customers, but we know where the spare key is. I get it out, find the fresh black bread and butter.

On the way down from home, when the mess boys went to fill up the big boiler, they found three frankfurters floating inside, boiled to bursting. A forgotten midnight snack. Klaus went crazy trying to find out who had done it. He said he could taste frankfurters in the coffee and

in everything for weeks. Just the slight taste of them, no matter how much we scrubbed out the boiler. It drove him mad.

I find the slow-cooked pork neck, the pickled cabbage. With mayonnaise and caperberries and pickled cucumber and cabbage, our pork sandwiches are good. We sit at the red booth and eat. We hold our plates, we hold the table. We brace when we pitch and rest when we don't. We are on automatic, not even thinking about the storm, about the sounds of the water and wind and metal. And we don't talk now. We eat until it's all gone, until we are heavy and tired and satisfied.

Soren looks at me, mayonnaise on his cheek. He puts his head down on the table, closes his eyes.

'Should we go to bed?' he asks, his voice slurred.

I look at the watch on his wrist. Almost three a.m. I guess Leo will be up soon, but probably no one will make it to breakfast. It will be just sandwiches tomorrow. Sandwiches and coffee sent round. Light breakfast for crew. Bread and cheese.

I feel relief wash over me. It will be an easy day for us, too rough to cook. An easy day.

Down in our passage, the fire chain still swings, but it's not touching the bulkhead for very long now. Maybe sleep will be possible.

'Goodnight, old man,' I say to Soren.

He salutes, his eyes closed against the bright light. I watch him fall into his cabin. *Happy birthday*, I think.

Tomorrow, I will tell everyone. Tomorrow, we will do something to celebrate.

It's only been a few months, but I feel like I have known him all my life. I can't remember anything before this.

21

WHEN THE NIGHT COMES

He salutes, his eyes closed against the bright light
I watch him fall into his cabin. Happy Sweden, I think.
Tomorrow I will tell everyone. Tomorrow, we will do
something to celebrate.
It's only been a few months, but I feel like I have known
him all my life. I can't remember anything before this.

Aalborg Harbour, Denmark
3rd July 1986

'Our home for the next nine months,' a voice says.

I turn. Standing there next to me is a young man.
A stranger. He is wearing the same uniform as me – a
chief steward apprentice.

'Soren,' he says. 'My name is Soren,' and he shakes my
hand. A strong shake, familiar somehow.

'I've seen you around,' he says.

I look at his face, at his blue, clear eyes. He is younger
than me, maybe early twenties. I nod although I doubt he
would ever have seen me. I don't remember him.

'How lucky,' he says. 'I heard a lot about her and I knew
instantly that I would very much like to be going.'

He is looking up at the ship now, and so am I. She looks
so big against the wharf, but she will feel small once we
are out there on the ocean with all of us crammed inside.

'Lucky. We are lucky,' he says. 'Can you believe it?' And
he slaps my arm, like a brother would, maybe, like an old
friend, and I nod. 'Yes,' I say, 'it's great.'

He keeps on talking. He doesn't seem to mind or even notice that I am silent. He just keeps on talking, blue eyes burning.

'I have had three contracts with J. Lauritzen before this one. Two reefer ships and an oil rig in the North Sea. I came to some Mediterranean ports, Israel, lots of European ports, Central America and Chile. The oil rig was boring. Three weeks on, three weeks off. Twelve hours, day in day out, all the while going nowhere, so you can imagine how exciting that was!'

I nod again and he goes on. He talks flat out. He tells me that there have only ever been two chief stewards on this ship, a father and his son. He tells me he has a camera, a good one, and he is going to take photos of everything. Everything. Black and white, arty, classic.

'Christ!' he says. 'Antarctica.'

Maybe I am glad of the company. Maybe it is just nice to have someone talk the way he does, on and on, so that I don't have to think, or worry, or wonder what I should be doing with myself. I can just listen – I can just get carried away with the stories.

I will be second cook and there will be nine long months working with this man, young and happy as he is. Against all my best intentions, I'm smiling now.

I have this feeling everything in my life is about to change forever, that things will never be the same. I know it's not too late to pull out, to go back to my island and get a job on a small fishing vessel, like I have done many

times before. I can stay where I am, stay still. I don't need to be sailing all the way to Antarctica. Maybe I don't need to go.

But when I look up, all I can see is the bright red of her hull, and there high on her bow is her name, painted in white. Words I have known all my life: *Nella Dan*.

'Christ!' Soren says again, and he nudges me with his elbow. 'We are lucky.'

MID-TIDE

Getting on the ferry was different every day. It depended on the tides. When the tide was high, the water lapped up on the concrete and tried to wet our feet, tried to grab our legs, and the ferry had to pull up right against the concrete because most of the jetty was under water. It was hard to get on the ferry then, and Peter would pull us all on board, one by one.

Sometimes we were late for school because it was rough and the crossing was slow. When it was *really* rough, when there were whitecaps and waves, we would play a game where you had to stand in the middle of the ferry with your feet together and your hands up in the air not touching anything. You had to try not to fall down. Whoever could stand like that for the longest time would win the game. I really liked that game – I liked the feeling of balancing high up on the water, of moving with it, like you were part of the ferry, like my body was part of its body, sailing on the cold water.

When the tide was low, the ferry couldn't pull right up along the wharf and had to stop at the very end of the jetty. It sat low in the water and we had to jump from the jetty down to the deck. Sometimes it was slippery. Sometimes it felt like a long way to jump – a leap of faith. My brother really hated that.

The only time it was easy to get on the ferry was when it was mid-tide. When the tide was perfectly in the middle of low and high, when everything was balanced.

Mid-tide made us all relax. When it was a mid-tide you knew it was going to be a good day. I would always hope for mid-tide, but it didn't happen that often.

The water was different every day and mid-tide came when you least expected it.

A GIANT AT THE TABLE

We were near the outskirts of the city and my brother wasn't walking slowly like usual – his blue sneakers were right there, keeping up with my white ones. I kept my hand on the money in my pocket, on the twenty-dollar note.

It was so much money.

Mum had never even asked for change or anything, and I didn't know how much movie tickets cost, but I was sure that there would be some money left over for a drink or maybe something to share, like popcorn.

I didn't mind going with my brother. He was keeping up and I knew that he was probably smiling. I didn't look across to see. I could just feel him there, and that was good.

We saw a movie called *Beat Street*. My brother chose it and it was the best movie I had ever seen. It was full of music, full of dancing. There was only one scary bit when one of the main characters got electrocuted on the train tracks near the end. I had never seen a film where anyone died before. He left behind a young baby.

He was a graffiti artist and he had painted some great work on the grey walls of the busted-up city in the movie. Somewhere in New York. Maybe the Bronx. A big city made of bare concrete.

He made the city look better.

After the movie, the walk back home wasn't so long, it wasn't tiring. We were carried along by the energy of the movie, the music, the freedom. At the old sweetshop on Hampden Road, we stopped and looked in the window at all the jars of flavoured sweets. Jars and jars filled with bright pink and green apple drops, red-striped sticks of candy, soft yellow squares coated with powdered sugar. My mouth watered.

My brother turned away from the window. He told me that he was going to start doing graffiti, not on walls or anything, just on paper.

'Maybe in a notebook.'

He was quiet then, until we were near our street.

'I can't draw very well,' he said and looked down at his sneakers. 'But maybe I can do this and it doesn't matter. Maybe I can just do it and no one can say it's wrong.'

I ran my hand along the fences as we walked, the picket fences, the brick walls. Bees hovered above a lavender bush, and there were roses a colour I'd never seen before. Almost pink and almost violet but not quite either – just somewhere soft in between.

'No one can say it's wrong,' I said.

* * *

When we got inside there was a giant in our house. He was sitting at the kitchen table, his chair pushed out so that his long legs could fit. Mum was sitting opposite him, her chair close to the table, her small yellow teacup in her hand with the matching yellow saucer in front of her.

My brother and I stood by the door and Mum said, 'This is Bo.'

The man stood up. 'Hello,' he said in a deep voice. 'How was the movie?'

My brother walked over to the table and sat down.

'We saw *Beat Street*,' he said. 'It was excellent.'

There was a plate of biscuits on the table. Scotch Finger. My brother was looking at them. I don't know where they came from. We didn't have any biscuits that morning.

I put my hand in my pocket, felt the change that was there. I pulled it out. One note and a few coins. I walked over and put it on the table near Mum. I could feel the man looking at me.

'Say hello,' Mum said.

'Hello.'

'Hello, Isla,' the man said.

I don't know how he knew my name or how he knew Mum, but when he sat down again, I tried not to look at him, but I did look at him, at his face, and his eyes were grey-blue like the sea.

THE WALNUT TREE

Out in the garden, I showed Bo the walnut tree. He smoked a cigarette.

'I like walnuts,' he said. 'I like to eat them when I walk.'

I thought about how my brother and I would use a rock to smash the walnuts open against the concrete steps at the back of the house and the pieces of nut would shatter and mix with the shell if you hit them too hard with the rock.

'How do you open them?' I asked.

'Ah,' he said, and he held one in his hand. 'It is very simple. See how one side, this pointy side, is all closed up?'

I nodded. The pointy side was sealed very tightly.

'But here on the other side, the round side, there is this spongy bit where the walnut hangs on the tree.'

I could see it. A dark vein between the two halves of the walnut shell.

'Like a skull,' I said.

'Yes,' he said. 'A little skull.'

He got a pocketknife out from his jeans. Shiny silver – stainless steel.

'My father gave me this knife,' he said, 'a long time ago,' and he pulled the sharp blade out from its tight hiding space. He held the walnut in one hand and pushed the knife into the soft cork vein with ease. Then he twisted the blade. There was a cracking sound, the nut opening – two halves there in his hand.

He held up the open half. 'A little brain,' he said.

The nut sat in one half of its shell in one whole piece, unbroken – complete. He took the nut out and gave it to me and I chewed up the warm taste. The creamy flesh tinged with the acid of the thin walnut skin, and together those tastes were delicious.

'I think we cannot be stopping now,' he said, already cracking open another nut and eating it whole.

'When I was at school, I used to steal walnuts from my neighbour. He had three big trees in a row. He was an old man called Emil. Maybe he was crazy, I don't know. I never saw him collect any of the nuts, but it was wrong to take them. I knew that. I'd eat them on the way to school, using this knife. I couldn't stop eating them once I started.'

Bo passed his knife to me.

'You try,' he said.

I picked up a walnut and held it in the palm of my hand. The knife felt heavy and warm and I slid the blade in carefully, the way Bo had shown me. I twisted the knife, my whole wrist turning with it, and there was a crack, the

shell came apart. The two halves were perfect, but the inside of the shell was dark. It was empty.

There was nothing there.

I looked at the space where the nut should have been. I turned my head and looked up at Bo.

'Oh,' he said, and he took the shell out of my hands, inspected it closely. 'The fairies ate that one.'

He handed me back the two halves of shell.

'You should keep it,' he said. 'Good luck.' He winked at me.

I looked at the shell again. I didn't know if it was true or not, if a shell could be good luck, but I put it in my pocket anyway. I kept it.

The next one I tried had a nut inside, but it split in half with the shell. It looked like a little heart. A skull with a little heart inside.

'Walnuts are very good for you,' Bo said. 'Very good.'

He smiled and cracked open another. We sat there and ate as many as we could find, twenty or more, one by one, until all around us were opened walnut shells in perfect halves.

THINGS I LOVE

We didn't have a lawnmower. Once a month the man from
next door would mow our backyard. He liked mowing, he
said. He would always do it early on a Saturday morning.
I didn't mind because I was always up. My brother and I
would get up early to watch the cartoons. They finished at
nine a.m., so if you didn't get up, you missed them. After
the cartoons came hours and hours of sports shows.

Mum would stay in bed and she wouldn't get up even
though the sound of the lawnmower was very loud and
would have woken her.

Bo stood by the back door and watched the man mow.

'Isn't it great?' he said to me when I came outside.
I nodded but I didn't know why. I didn't know what was
great. When the man finished and left our garden, Bo ran
down the concrete steps and got down on the grass. He
rolled around, over and over, and when he stopped rolling
he lay on his belly in the middle of the lawn.

My brother came out to see what was happening and we

walked down the steps and stood at the edge of the grass together. He was already sniffing and my eyes had started to itch with all the bits of grass in the air. Bo put his face to the earth, breathed in deep and he stayed like that for ages. When he looked up, the grass had made imprints on his face and he said, 'I love grass!' It made us laugh, we didn't know why. 'I love it,' he said again and he rolled over and got up. His white T-shirt was all stained by the freshly cut grass.

'I feel like I haven't smelt grass since I was a boy.'

'I get hayfever,' my brother said and he rubbed his eyes, then started to sneeze. Bo took us inside and he washed my brother's face with a hot face washer.

'Do you think your T-shirt is wrecked?' my brother asked when he had stopped sneezing. 'Mum says grass doesn't come out.'

Bo looked down at his stained T-shirt, brown with dirt and green with grass.

'It's perfect,' he said. 'My T-shirt is perfect.'

A BOX OF CHEWING GUM

It was something special to go on Bo's ship. It was something I had imagined, looking at all the ships that were on the wharf and thinking that I'd love to see what it was like inside. Sometimes there were open days for navy ships, but they were not like *Nella*. They were grey and clean and organised. Compartmentalised.

Mum took us down to the wharf on a Sunday. It was the day before Bo was leaving again for Antarctica. For Casey.

Nella Dan was waiting for us when we got there, all bright and warm. Inside, she was bigger than you expected. There were stairs and many floors and cabins and corridors and outside decks and undercover decks and showers and bathrooms and places to eat and places to sit and all of them felt cosy and comforting and lived in and loved. It was like she came from some other time and some other place. A place much better than here.

Bo made us lunch and we sat with the crew at their table. They put cushions on our chairs so we could reach. And

we were like tiny people, like fairies, and everything was giant. The glasses of milk and the litre bottles of beer and the slices of dark bread and cheese. A man called Soren, who had long yellow hair, drank a whole litre of milk right out of the carton and then he burped loudly and laughed. It made my brother laugh too. He really laughed.

Later, when we were finished lunch, Soren lifted my brother up high off the ground so that he could see all the boxes of duty-free lollies and chocolates that were stacked on top of a tall storage cupboard. Soren told him to choose whatever he liked in a thick accent that was deep and rolling and happy. I saw my brother's hands grab an orange box. I saw his eyes, how big they were. When Soren put him back down on the ground, my brother looked up at him and asked if it was okay. Soren patted him on the head and said something in Danish. Then everyone laughed and the crew all patted my brother as they passed by, as they went back to work.

We walked home from the wharf with Mum, and my brother held the box tightly all the way. It was a box of a hundred packets of Wrigley's chewing gum, and even though I had never seen my brother eat chewing gum before, I knew he still couldn't believe his luck.

He looked at me and he told me that I could have half, that we could share the chewing gum. That's how things were between us.

MS *Nella Dan*
Voyage 2, 1986/1987 Season
29th October 1986
Position: 56° 39.000' S, 147° 14.000' E
Captain's note: Making good speed on the way to Casey, and planning for the resupply continues.

> *They come out of the soft grey*
> *White with clean black lines*
> *Albatross, gliding clear*
> *They turn with no effort and rarely beat their wings*
> *Metres of soft feathers stretched out*
> *Yet against the endless water on all sides*
> *They look small.*

Four a.m. and even though there are many of us in the galley, we are quiet – half-sleeping. Still separated by the solitude that night brings. It takes time to readjust.

But we are focused. Busy. One task and then another.

Coffee in my cracked cup, black and bitter. It pulses through me, fills my empty stomach, and my thoughts

quicken. My eyes moisten and blink and I am rising up. I am coming into the working day.

The working day.

Leo has been here for hours already baking. The life of a baker. The galley warm with the smell of bread, with the smell of pastries coming out of the oven to be cooled and glazed. He always gives us one if we want it, the custard inside still hot. You have to be careful or you will burn the roof of your mouth and then enjoy nothing for the rest of the day.

Sweetness in the air and now there is sweetness in my belly. I feel the sugar pushing my blood around my body. Soon the air will be thick with the smell of bacon frying. Black pudding. Salt and butter and meat and eggs.

We prep for the breakfast rush. We will not eat again until it is over and the cleaning is done. Peel and boil and mash the potatoes ready for the potato cakes. Cut up the grapefruits, open and slice the tinned pears, put out the cereals that the Australians like to eat. Corn Flakes, Sultana Bran, muesli with milk. Then the sliced cheeses, the ham, the smoked salmon.

Five-thirty a.m. already. The seamen are up and thermoses of coffee have been set out for them. They have their coffee and then start work. At seven they will come back in, hungry for their cooked breakfast.

The mess boys have overslept. They are young, seventeen. Just boys. They fight the heaviness of sleep and lose.

Heavy bones, the weight of all that growth needing rest and fighting the morning. Always fighting.

Erik finally appears, his uniform crumpled and a little stained, his hair sticking up. He does not speak but leans up in the corner near the ovens, his eyes squinting with the fluoro light.

Klaus tells him to go and fix his hair and then get the breakfast room set up and to wake Jonas up 'for Christ's sake!'

Erik leaves the galley, stomping slowly, and reappears in a few minutes with his blond hair wet from being slicked down with water.

'Jonas is coming,' he says.

I smile at him and he smiles back, his awkward front teeth squashed together. He is trying to grow a moustache but his hair is too fine and he is too young and it looks like there are crumbs left behind on the top of his lip, which you want to wipe away. But he is a good kid, and he works hard and mostly he does not complain. And every one of us knows exactly what it feels like to be seventeen, on your first ship, working fourteen-hour shifts, so very far away from home.

Aalborg Harbour, Denmark
3rd July 1986

I can hear a woman crying. I turn. A young man – a boy – is standing tall. A mother holds on to him for dear life, her arms in a thick brown coat around his sides.

'It's too far,' she says. 'It won't be safe.'

He doesn't answer. He is looking down at the concrete. Maybe he is embarrassed – maybe he is trying not to cry, I don't know.

Why do you have to go?

I was sixteen, leaving. My first ship. My grandmother had packed food and a thermos of coffee for the ferry. She held on to my face, held my cheeks so hard it almost hurt. She looked in my eyes and told me I had promised I would never go.

'You said you hated the sea,' she said.

I could never explain to her in one hundred years that

everything inside of me had changed and that I had to go now and that I did not know why.

The boy takes a small step back and the mother lets him go.

'It will be fine. I will be fine. I promise,' he tells her.

The woman covers her face with her hands now. I can see how she shakes. The boy leans over and speaks softly into her ear. I cannot hear the words. Maybe he is telling her not to worry. Maybe he is telling her that he loves her. That he is sorry for leaving.

I'm sorry.

Forgive me.

My grandmother. She kissed my cheek, turned away from me and walked with her slow, serious walk, the walk she had my whole life. I watched her go. She did not wait for the ferry to pull away and she did not look back, not even once.

I was alone then. I saw my island, a place I had never left on my own, become very small and then disappear altogether into the vast Baltic Sea. I went inside and sat down on a plastic chair and I did not look outside again for the many hours it took to reach the huge wharf outside of Copenhagen. I had made my choice.

* * *

Someone nudges my arm. It's Soren, standing next to me. He rubs his hands together. 'Here we go,' he says. 'Antarctica!'

I walk up the gangway, look back to see the boy kiss his mother on the cheek and then run, all long arms and legs until he is standing right behind me.

'Hi,' he says.

'Hi,' I say, and I can see his lip quiver ever so slightly. He tells me his name is Erik.

I look at his face, at the way his hair hangs over his forehead, and how his teeth are long like horses' teeth. I want to tell him that by the time we reach the equator, the crew will be a tight family unit, the ship our island – and home will not be such a painful thing to think on.

I shake his hand. 'Hi, Erik,' I say.

MS *Nella Dan*
Voyage 2, 1986/1987 Season
1st November 1986
Position: 61° 59.000' S, 118° 9.000' E
Captain's note: Today King Neptune arrived to anoint those who had not travelled below 60 degrees south. The bergy bits and icebergs are getting more prevalent as we edge our way closer to Casey.

Bits of ice hit the hull of the ship, like giant hailstones on a tin roof – clip, clip, clip. The ship crunches through small patches of ice. Cape petrels and snow petrels glide outside my porthole.

I fall asleep in my bunk to the sound of the ice against the ship.

I am tired. I feel the heaviness in my face, in my bones. Even Soren keeps asking me if I am all right. It is the bags under my eyes.

We are only a day from Casey but the ice is getting thicker – multi-seasoned ice all joined together – and we slush through at a slow speed. When I lie in my bunk I can hear the ice pushed right up against the hull, the ship quaking with the strain of the engine working overtime to give us enough push.

Sometimes there is a scraping sound of a sharp piece, a growler – scratching *Nella* – hurting her. No matter how tired I am, that sound always wakes me. It is like I have known it all my life. Like the howl of a wolf. It is one of those sounds that wakes every cell in my body and says, be alert. Wake up!

But then it is past and my muscles relax, my heart slows down. I think, maybe I should just get up, make some coffee. Then I am fast asleep again – out cold. There are no dreams, no twilight, just my alarm going off suddenly when I least expect it. A ringing from far away – getting louder and louder. A sound that won't go away.

STANDING IN THE
PHONE BOX

With a handful of twenty-cent pieces in my pocket, my brother and I would walk from our house on Mona Street down along Francis Street to the main road, to the phone box there.

I never saw anyone else use that phone box for all the time we lived in that house. But we would use it, every second Sunday. We'd both squeeze in and shut the folding glass door behind us, and I'd have butterflies in my stomach and maybe my brother would too. Maybe I was scared and maybe he was too.

He'd hold the receiver and I'd put three twenty-cent pieces in and dial the number – the STD code for Victoria and then the seven numbers that came after.

My brother would say, 'It's ringing!' and hold the phone up to me like the receiver was burning his face. He'd look worried, so I'd take it from him.

When someone picked up on the other end, three small beeps would come down the line, then a 'hello'. It would be Dad's voice and I'd get a shock, then I'd say, 'Hello – it's me,' all while my brother watched me to see if it was okay. If I was okay. To see if we were in trouble or not.

'How's school? How's your brother?'

'Good. He's fine. He's here. I'll put him on.'

When my brother took the receiver, I'd put in the remaining twenty-cent pieces, hear them slotting down the metal insides of the phone.

Time would go fast then. The time would run, and the phone would start to beep and we'd say, 'We have to go,' and say goodbye. Dad would say, 'I'll just keep talking until the phone cuts off.'

Sometimes that would feel like ages and sometimes it would be no time at all, and then he was gone, ripped away, and it was just my brother and me standing in the phone box with the phone beeping because the call had been cut off.

Dad was gone. He was far away and we lived on an island now. We'd hang the phone up, open the door and walk home together, without talking.

THE WHITE VAN

I waved goodbye to Peter and we stepped off the ferry.

'See you in the morning,' he said.

The wood of the jetty was slippery with green slime. It was rotting, and we had to be careful. I didn't know what I would do if I fell in, if my brother fell in. Sometimes there were huge orange starfish all the way down on the concrete bottom. Starfish bigger than my head. But mostly you couldn't see anything but the dense surface, watch the sludge and rubbish circle around, taste the rank smell of it in your mouth.

The water at the wharf was never able to wash itself clean.

My brother asked if we could go past the boat park, but I just wanted to walk home the quickest way, and not go all the way around the headland. I told him he could go on his own.

'You're old enough, aren't you?' I said.

He didn't answer. He looked down at the ground and I walked off. I walked fast and I didn't turn back to see if he was following me until I got to the bottom of Kelly's steps.

My brother wasn't there. He was probably already at the park playing on the wooden pirate ship, climbing the ropes and going down the metal slide.

I trudged up the cold, worn steps and marched up Kelly Street. But on Francis Street I slowed down. I looked for flowers to pick – the ones that poked out of fences, in between the pickets or over the tops. Only the flowers that were leaning over the pavement – leaning onto common ground. Still, I was careful not to be seen. I checked up and down the street before I picked any. Lavender, white daisies, a yellow rose. I took my time, made a little bouquet and held it tightly in my hand.

The sun was going down already, slipping behind the mountain, and when I turned into Mona Street, I could see my brother standing by our gate. Something was wrong – I could see it in his face. A white van was revving down the street towards us and my brother started screaming out my name.

I ran, not really knowing why, but everything inside me told me to RUN. I got the key out of my pocket and tried to get the front door open quickly, but the key wouldn't go in, my fingers numb and tingling and useless, and the white van slowed down as it went past our house. It was like a film, like slow motion. I saw the man's face, the driver.

He was looking right at us, small eyes squinting, then the key found its way, slotted in, and the door pushed open. The van sped up and skidded around the corner, smoke burning off the tyres as it went.

We fell inside and slammed the red door behind us. We stood in the dark hallway together, our bodies up against the door. I was breathing hard. I looked at my hands. I must have dropped the flowers on the street somewhere. My brother told me that a man had started walking next to him and asked him if he wanted to go fishing.

'I said no thanks, but then I saw another man up ahead and he was looking at me. He was standing by that van with the door open.'

I felt very sick then. I felt something very cold inside my stomach.

'I ran away,' my brother said. 'I ran home, but I couldn't find you.'

We stayed leaning against the door for a long time. I don't know how long, but I knew that we were both listening for that van, that we would dream about it, look for it out of the corners of our eyes for the rest of the time we lived in Battery Point.

Battery Point, where the houses were old and solid like tombstones, and there were never any people on the streets or in the front gardens. There were never any people anywhere. Just my brother and me, walking fast, always looking behind us.

MS *Nella Dan*

Voyage 2, 1986/1987 Season

5th November 1986

Position: 66° 16.000' S, 110° 32.000' E

Captain's note: The Casey Station leader came on board to brief expeditioners and for final discussions prior to resupply commencing. The LARCs (Lighter Amphibious Resupply Craft) were discharged and cargo operations commenced with the first load of cargo departing the ship at 10.20 a.m. Key achievements have been to deploy marine science personnel to prepare for their summer campaign, and commencement of refuelling operations this morning. We have been pumping for approximately 7 hours and have transferred 178,000 litres.

A fourteen-hour day and I'm looking forward to sitting down and tasting the home brew at the base. My chance to go ashore – to Casey – Antarctica. To step onto the continent, to be part of it.

I get dressed, borrow some boots. My thermals are tight and itchy and it's hot waiting in the bunker room with my life jacket on, my hat, the thick gloves. But I am

looking forward to the night, the station handover, the party. Winterers coming out and the new crew going in.

'It's bigger than Christmas,' Klaus told me. 'Bigger than New Year's Eve.'

This chance to get low on the water, see penguins close up, stand under the big sky with ice all around me.

Ready.

The rope ladder ahead, the LARC below almost full but with room for three more crew. Just three. Soren and Erik and me.

'Don't drink too much!' Benny yells out from behind me. 'I'm not going to carry anyone up the ladder, if you drink too much.'

Crew from the LARC give it back, laughing. 'Hey! We are young, not like you.'

'Old Man of the Sea.'

I catch his eye and he smiles and I like him, Benny. Always clean-shaven. His face lined with salt and sun and with the cold, and none of us know how old he is, how long he has been at sea. Maybe forever. His eyes are green and they move like mist over the water. Searching. He sees everything.

'Ready?' he says.

He checks my life jacket and holds on to me as I step down backwards over the edge. My big boot finds the first rung and the ladder swings out with my weight.

'Make the most of it.'

Benny is still holding my jacket with his strong hand.

I might never get another chance.

I step down another rung. The ladder slaps back hard against the ship. I hold on, watch that my fingers don't get crushed between the ladder and the cold steel hull. We are riding high in the water, most of the heavy cargo offloaded, half the fuel delivered. It's a long way down. I grip the ropes. I step down. The ladder moves, the ship moves, the LARC below me moves. I'm almost there.

'Hey!'

Above, a head pokes over the side. It's one of the apprentice deck boys, Per is his name. He talks to Benny, a small voice, and the wind has picked up now, but I can hear enough of what he is saying.

'Need a cook to stay . . . refuelling team . . . eleven p.m. break. Soup. Sandwiches.'

Benny looks down at me, his face still. My legs begin to move up the ladder, step by step, rung by rung, until I'm back at the top. I let go of the guide ropes, stand up straight and look down over the edge. Most of the crew are staring up at me. I raise my hand in a wave. Soren and Erik wave back.

'We'll bring you a beer if we don't drink it all!' Soren yells, and they are away. The LARC pulls out, moves off towards Casey, towards land. I hear singing, laughing, the party already started. The sound carries across the ice-cold water.

'Maybe one of the LARC drivers can come and get you later,' Benny says. But we both know that won't happen.

'Another time,' I say.

Another time.

Benny doesn't say any more. He is still again, his eyes on the LARC, and its wake is a straight shiny line pointing to land.

I step out of the little steel room and walk with my heavy boots, my life jacket still on. I go down the hall and into the passenger mess. I stand there for a while, I don't know why. It's not my place but I sit down on one of the chairs anyway.

The ship is almost empty now. A ghost ship. A few men on the bridge, some below. The captain. And Benny – our bosun. A few men asleep, a few on watch, one man resting after a cargo chain snapped and smashed his hand. He has been given some painkillers and sent to rest. No one knew if his hand was broken but Benny said it was bad. He said that when it happened it sounded like the bones shattered like glass. Klaus sent up a packet of frozen peas to help with the pain. That was all frozen peas were good for, he said. He hated peas.

It was something about the way his mother had boiled them, pale and soggy. He never forgot the taste – that smell, of soft boiled peas on his plate going cold.

A small boy sitting there in the night refusing to eat his peas no matter how much his mother begged.

'I'll tell your father when he gets home,' she'd say. But his father was far away at sea, perhaps on this very ship. He would be away for months and months, and by the time he

got home, the peas would be long forgotten. His mother would just be relieved. Everyone would just be happy.

Outside, through the portholes, it is light like a clear early morning.

I look up at the clock on the wall. It stopped at 6.24 somewhere out on the Indian Ocean. I don't know if it was a.m. or p.m. but Jens, the engineer, said he couldn't work out how the hell to fix it. He had tried twice. There are faint grease marks next to the clock where he had leant his engineer's hands on the bulkhead while trying to get it down.

'I'll be damned if I can bloody fix that clock,' he said, and he shrugged his shoulders, walked away. He had better things to do, important things to fix – engine parts, hot, moving parts that had to keep working so that the ship could keep running. Jens had no time to be messing with dead clocks.

I know I should just go to bed, get some rest for a few hours before I have to prepare the sandwiches. My body is heavy, rocking with some kind of internal motion. I feel displaced.

I put my head down on the table. The damask tablecloths are new and clean and I can smell the stiff fabric. I stare at the sauce bottles in their little wooden compartments – the tomato sauce, the HP sauce, the salt, the pepper, the mustard. This mess, where so many expeditioners have sat, day after

day, year after year, season on season. Breakfast, lunch and dinner, puddings and movie screenings and nightcaps. Then over. Over. The daily menu typed and ready. Eggs and bacon, black pudding, pastries, coffee/tea, juice. Consommé, pommes frites, lamb cutlets, cheese and biscuits. Roast pork, honeyed carrots, salad, cabbage and butter beans, potato gratin, sponge cake, apple cake, preserved fruits.

The hot, crowded galley, that broken clock on the wall, the tape player that chewed all the best tapes, my hair always smelling like roasted meats, like browned butter, like salty pork crackling. Tonight, all these weeks in, I just wanted to step onto the solid frozen earth and say, *I am here*. Only a cook, but here all the same.

My eyes start to close, my body warm in the thermals and jacket and outer pants and boots, and I know that if I don't get up this very minute I will fall asleep right here, my head resting on the tablecloth, my nostrils filled with the sweet sickly smell of tomato sauce.

Get up.

Get up!

I make myself stand, walk, one foot in front of the other, big boots clumping and my outer gear swishing as I walk down the stairs to the Swamp, to my cabin. Inside – dark, snug, my washed socks hanging on the elastic clothes line. I take my life jacket off, sit with my travel clock in my hands. It is 7.20 p.m. If I get up at ten, that will leave enough time.

I lie on my bunk, face first. I close my eyes.

Tomorrow, in the morning, the expeditioners will say, 'Thanks for the breakfast. Danish bacon is so good!' and I will nod and smile and say, 'Thank you. Thanks so much. Have a good day.' I will clean up and start preparing the lunch and soon, when the resupply is done, *Nella* will pull away from Casey, move out of the harbour and pass the small island filled with seabirds so incredible. Out of the grime-stained porthole above the sink I will watch it slip away and it will be gone before I've finished the dishes.

MS *Nella Dan*
Voyage 2, 1986/1987 Season
7th November 1986
Position: 66° 16.000' S, 110° 32.000' E
Captain's note: Refuelling continues. Weather holding.

> *Ice sparkles in the sun*
> *Like diamonds — like jewels, thousands of them shining*
> * in the white*
> *Beyond — the blue dark water*
> *Above — the blue light sky*
> *And out in the bay — the red of my ship*
> *Red against the sea, the sky*
> *Red against the ice*
> *Red there, calling out to me.*
> *Don't stay away too long.*

I sit down on a worn couch and drink my coffee. It isn't
very good, milk and too much sugar, but I don't mind.
Someone made it for me and that's enough. I will drink it.
I will enjoy it, sitting here in this room. Casey — Antarctica.

Antarctica. Inside, looking out.

Benny found me after breakfast and said I could go across, visit the station. 'Just a few hours.' My prize for missing the party.

Opposite me, there are two men asleep in chairs, magazines open on their laps. One is snoring, softly. He has a thick red beard even though the long hair on his head is brown. It is impressive, this beard. The beard of a winterer – a long cold year of solid effort. Sometimes my father would come home with a beard like this, strange and rough, and I would not recognise him after he had been away for so long. I would look at him from a distance, study him from the doorway. Wonder who this strange man was who knew me so well. Was it really him? My father, with brown hair like mine, but on his face a beard of red clear to see. Red – bright like fire. Red – bright like flames.

I touch my own face, feel the stubble on my chin. I can never grow a beard like that, not full. My beard would not keep my skin warm in the cold. I only need to shave once a week, and that is something at sea.

I look over at the pile of magazines on the coffee table near the sleeping men. I want to get one, to read some old news from the world, but I stay put. I don't want to wake anyone. They have been working hard, their hands stained from the resupply. So I just sit. I take it in. I drink this strange coffee. I look around.

It feels lived in, the room. Stuffed full of life.

In the evenings, men crammed in, seats hard to find. Some stand by the pool table, some at the bar. There

is laughter and there are arguments, there is joy, there is wanting. The mundane, day-to-day, all here in this room. The years here, in the corners and against the walls, years walked into the faded carpet.

The echoes of men.

The sun hits my face. My eyes follow the rays to the glass of the square windows. There, beyond the brightness, I can see a hill made of stones. Brown against the white. Brown, the colour of the earth, so out of place. A kingdom of rocks in the snow and in the ice.

Something inside me kicks alive, stings – like memory. Familiar. Real. I stand, move closer to the window. I keep looking at the hill. A hill of stones. A hill of rocks.

Something hits the floor, a magazine, and the man with the red beard wakes. He stretches his arms, his eyes surprisingly green and young and wide. He looks at me.

'Hi,' he says.

'Hi,' I say.

He picks the magazine up off the floor and puts it on the table. He stretches out again, stands up.

I look to the window. 'What is this place?' I ask, and I point at the hill, to the stones. The man comes closer, squints into the light.

'Reeves Hill,' he says, and he stares with me for a while at the scene out there. Then he looks at his watch.

'Time for lunch,' he says.

I follow him up the tunnel to the mess. He tells me his name is Ben. He is a diesel mechanic and he's been up

all night watching the fuel lines. We shake hands and his grip is strong. Welcoming. I still have my coffee cup in my other hand, almost empty, but I can't drink anymore.

The mess is full, most people already eating. It's not large but there is room enough. The summer crew are sitting together. I wave to them – I know most by name from the journey down. Not yet grease-stained, not yet calloused, not yet comfortable in this new place. What will it be like when the darkness comes? When the cold dark is pressing down on these small rooms, on these thin walls.

I have this sudden feeling that *Nella* has left, sailed away without me. I can't see her. I am far away, left behind. I want to run, to see if she's there in the bay. I want to go back to my ship, my home. I do not belong here. But someone calls my name. I look across the room. It's a solid grey-bearded man. The station leader. He waves me over to his table, asks me to join him. And the feeling is gone. I know the resupply is all still going and *Nella* is out there. Half a day of work at least. She won't leave me here.

'Have you had a good look around?' he asks me, and I tell him, 'Yes, thank you. I have had a good look around. Inside.'

He is sitting with the winterers. A group bound together. They are almost home, their time over. But for now this is still their house. They are comfortable – many just in their long thermal underwear and socks, glazed eyes, cheeks sunburnt to the colour of blood, eating with gusto. Beef casserole and pasta, fresh vegetables that have been missing

for so long. Full bowls of fruit salad on the tables waiting to be devoured. Fresh fruit, eaten in silence – fresh fruit eaten with reverence. With cream, with ice-cream. Fresh fruit.

The station leader nudges me. 'Won't you eat something?' he asks. His eyes are dark and ancient and tired.

I pat my stomach. 'No, I'm fine,' I tell him.

He looks at me, serious now. 'Just say when you want to go back.'

I nod. 'Thank you.' Then I ask him about the stones. The hill. I ask if I can go over to see it. If I can go outside.

He narrows his eyes, looks confused. Maybe I have said the name wrong. 'Reeves Hill?'

'I don't have anyone who can take you,' he says, but then he pauses, like he can see something in me, something in my eyes, urgent. Burning.

'I suppose you can go over if you're careful.'

I smile. 'Maybe nice to go outside,' I say.

He nods. Nods again. 'Yes,' he says. 'All right. Follow the road around then look for the track. Don't wander off. Melt everywhere right now. Cracks in the ice, lakes of water under it. Just follow the road and the track until you're on the rocks.'

'Okay,' I say, already standing. Already there in my mind.

'Put your name on the board. Be back in an hour. I don't want to have to come looking for you.'

'Thank you,' I say. I shake his hand, almost run out of the mess. I try not to look at anyone in case they stop me.

In case they say, 'Sorry, you can't go.' But then I see Ben and he waves. He stands up, holds out a pair of sunglasses.

'Take these,' he says.

I take them.

I move down the tunnel towards the doors, towards the sun. I write my name on the blackboard, *Bo — Nella Dan*, then I put *11.50 a.m.* under TIME in white chalk. I find a freezer suit, orange and padded, and I struggle to get it on, get zipped up. It's roasting hot inside the suit, but when I open the heavy metal doors, I feel the cold — that bite on my face, slicing into my lungs — and I put my hat on, then Ben's sunglasses and suddenly the brightness does not hurt my eyes. I can see it all clearly, in full spectrum. All the full-colour glory and the insides of me are soaring.

I follow the road, my big boots crunching in the loose frozen dirt. Summer. Minus one degree, but that sun is streaming down, melting everything on the surface, slick and slippery.

The sound of the resupply echoes all around — the truck engines, the cranes, the *beep, beep, beep* of reversing machines. A hive of engines working around the clock until the resupply is done. But as I move closer to the hill, get further down the road, the silence starts to win. I can feel it come down over me, over the place like double-glazing. My breath loud, my heart beating in all this cold silence.

The hill of stones is there, ahead. I'm getting closer.

My foot slips out from under me and I land hard. I'm on the ground, still. Black ice. I didn't see it on the road

but I can see it now. I try to feel if anything is wrong, if anything hurts. What would happen if I broke something? How long would I have to wait? How cold would I get? I look up at the blue sky, no clouds now, only slight streaks of translucent grey and pink. I get up slowly and breathe. I'm just winded. I tell myself to walk slower, to be careful.

No need to rush, no need to end your season early and be sent home. But part of me wants to run, get to the hill as fast as I can. It's like someone is waiting for me up there, something important that I might miss.

A hill of stones – a hill made of stones.

The road ends.

A line of ice to cross, covered in thick crystals, hard snow that never melts in this cold dryness. I can see footprints, tracks to follow where people have been. The snow is deep and crisp right up to my knees and it's hard to walk. Lines of penguin tracks crisscross the human path, little feet skimming across the top surface of frozen white with ease. Little feet waddling, not plodding. Little feet dancing, not sinking down like my heavy feet.

I plod on, step by step, sinking down. I keep going and when I look up, I can see flashes of white against the sky, against the rocks. Flashes of white, the air alive with them. Tiny pure white birds, here at the end of the earth. Snow petrels. A nesting ground.

The ice thins. The rocks begin, like a desert, brown and dry. I take my hat off, let my head feel the cold air. I'm hot, but I keep climbing. I can see the nests in the rocks

all around. Baby snow petrels somewhere safe inside. Safe and warm somehow. Babies so small, so perfect and white. I'm careful not to get too close, not to disturb them. I keep walking up, away from the nests, and when I reach the top the view hits me with full force. The whole of the rich blue bay, still. Perfect. *Nella Dan* there in her spot, reflecting red off the water. The sky cloudless. Giant white cliffs running on and on, then out to the horizon, icebergs lined up for all of time, blue and brilliant white taking up the whole scene. Every blue that there is — that exists. One million shades of blue and white. The scale of it all measured against me, one man standing here. Just one man, small and breathless.

I find a big flat rock, sit down with this place humming through me. And they come. Snow petrels swoop down from the sky, arc in circles above my head.

I stay still, let them surround me, and all is silent except for the sound of wings beating against the cold air. Wings of snow-white feathers, these perfect creatures at home here in the strangeness of this place. So white they disappear when they fly over ice, invisible except for their small black eyes looking down, their black beaks pointing.

Papa — I am here.

A story told long ago. But I remember. The feel of my bed, and the smell of the feathers in my pillow. My father's voice, deep and far away, carrying me to a kingdom of ice. A hill made of stones.

'If you climb it, if you make the journey, you can see far into the distance. You can see the whole of the bay and the icebergs along the horizon. A vast city of icebergs stretching out for as far as you can see.

'Then, if you sit still, if you wait and are patient, the little angels come down from the sky and fly around you. They come so close, their wings almost touch the skin on your face. They come down to say *hello*.'

'Are they really angels, Papa?'

He touched my head with his warm hand. 'Time for sleep,' he said.

I closed my eyes and dreamt of falling snow that turned to pure white birds. I watched each snowflake fly away one by one, and I wished I had wings so that I could go with them. I wished that I could follow.

This place, alive and real. Just like he told me. Just like he said.

And I am here.

Papa, I am here.

THE SUN ON THE WALL

There in the dark attic room
A beam of light from the air vent projected the sky
I watched, my eyes wide, as a silent movie rolled out across
the wall
The clouds morphed and moved like grey smoke, weightless
A perfect orb of light grew bright – burned gold
And I could feel it
It was the sun
Rising – coming now
The night was over.

A HOUSE ON THE HILL

'We will be happy here,' she said, and I said yes.

A room of my own in the small white cottage on the hill. Closer to the sun – to the light. Up high in West Hobart, looking down on the city. A little stone cottage of our very own, with no lodgers and just us – my brother and me and Mum and our new cat, Molly. A sunroom out the back with a glass wall that let in as much light as there was, and Mum hired a piano. We put it in the sunroom and I could play it after school. There was a new round table and four chairs, a tiny kitchen, a little balcony, stairs that led down to a brick courtyard and a square of lawn with red roses, and I thought – *yes, we will be happy here*.

We were going to a new school. A school with uniforms, and everything would be different.

'We will be happy here,' she said.

Darlington cottage.

It cost $53,000, which was almost all the money that Mum got from the settlement. Still, there was some left for

a car. A *car*, which was really something after not having one for so long. Part of the school fees came from a scholarship, and the rest was to be found somehow. It would be found.

Moving in.

Mum said it was the first house that had been hers, and that made her smile very much. My brother and I could feel it – that maybe things *would* be different now.

My room was painted sage green and it had a built-in bookshelf next to the fireplace. My brother's room was painted blue and he had a bunk bed. He decided to sleep on the top bunk.

And he was going to have a birthday party – his first real one. A birthday party in a house that we owned.

It was our home.

THE MOUNTAIN

Mum drove us up to the top of the mountain in the new car. Bo was back and he could only just fit in the front seat even though my brother and I were small enough for him to push his seat right back. The car only had two doors. You had to pull the passenger seat forward to get in and out of the back. But we had not had a car the whole time we had lived in Hobart and it was nice to feel the road underneath me and look out of the window. The road took us up slowly in wide circles of green to Fern Tree and then onto a steep rocky road where the trees thinned out until there were just shrubs and huge boulders and the sky, which was clear.

When we got to the top, Mum parked the car and we all got out. Bo stretched his legs. He jumped up and down on the spot and clapped his hands together.

'Cold up here,' he said.

My brother pulled his beanie out of his pocket and put it on. I zipped up my parka and put the hood over my head.

I had only been to the top of the mountain once, with school and we had walked there from Fern Tree. It was a long walk and it was very cold. We had to huddle away from the wind behind rocks and cook our lunch on Trangia stoves that ran on methylated spirits. We cooked two-minute noodles and ate them quickly and they were good but everything smelt a bit like metho. After lunch we were warmer and it was easier to walk the rest of the way up.

Our outdoor education teacher, Mr Janik, told us that the wind chill at the top of the mountain, even on a very sunny day, could take the temperature down by fifteen degrees and could cause hypothermia in no time.

'You lose most of your heat from your head,' he told us. 'You must protect your head.'

I asked Bo if he had a hat, but he said no.

'I am very used to the cold,' he said and he winked at me.

Past the car park, flat square rocks ran on like a giant's pavement and they went for as far as you could see. We started to walk on them, and up close the rocks had cracks and crevices large enough for shrubs to grow in and the surfaces were covered in circles of white and grey lichen. The sun was shining down on the rocks and that felt good. We walked on the rocks and looked down the mountain at Hobart and the river. It was a clear view, not like when I had come up with school. That day we had not been able to see anything but cloud, and the wind was so strong that you could lean right into it and not fall over.

Mum and my brother stopped walking after a few minutes and said they were going back to the car because Mum was cold. Bo and I kept walking. He walked easily on the giant rocks and I kept up. I had my walking boots on. Soon the crevices got big enough that we could jump down into them. It was like a maze of rocks and it was sheltered from the wind. I noticed that there were lizards on the rocks – skinks the colour of rust, eyes wide and still, trying to get warm.

Bo sat down in the sun and looked out towards the back of the mountain.

'You could easily get lost here,' he said.

'Yes,' I said. People did get lost up here. Sometimes they even died.

We didn't talk for a while after that. I wanted to ask him about the ship, about where they were going next and what it was like. But silence was easy with Bo. It was not lonely and I could think. I could think about the sky and about the light and how things changed. I could stop holding myself so very tightly.

'So, you are starting a new school – and your mum will be going to university,' he said.

I nodded.

'I know she is excited,' he said.

I looked out at the endless square shapes cracked and worn by a million years of wind and rain. The rock I sat on felt cold against my hands. I wondered how cold the rocks became at night, if the lichen on them froze and what happened to the skinks then. Where did they go at night?

Some of the stones were shaded by larger stones and they would never see the sun at all. They were hidden and stuck in the shadows. Never to be touched by the light.

'I guess we should go back,' Bo said and he stood up. He took my hand and helped me up and together we climbed out of the labyrinth.

Back on the flat slabs of granite, the wind had died down and it really did feel warmer now. We walked slowly to the car and I could see parts of the Derwent River below, reflecting the sun so brightly that it made me squint. The water looked like melted gold.

'I like this mountain,' Bo said. 'Denmark is very flat. But we are just small and there are mountains all around us. The countries around us are giant mountains and if we want to go to the mountains, well then we don't have very far to go. We just take a ferry and we are there – in the mountains.'

Bo started to laugh so hard then, and it made me laugh too, even though I didn't know what was so funny.

But I liked the mountain. It was nice to look up and see it when it wanted to be seen. Because it could disappear whenever it felt like it – be completely gone under thick cloud or fog, making Hobart flatter, greyer. And when the mountain re-emerged it would be different. Changed. Maybe dusted with snow – or just a dark raw shape – a face of long stones. But sometimes it would be golden with the sun – lit up under a blue open sky. Cold and clear and full of light, radiating out.

THIS IS COFFEE

'How do you drink that stuff?'

My mum poked her tongue out at Bo and told him
that she liked it. She heaped a teaspoon of the dry brown
granules into her little teacup. 'I like it,' she said again.

Bo shook his head.

'First, you don't own a whisk, now this!' He was smiling
and his voice was loud and happy. He waved me into the
small kitchen.

'Even a child will know,' he said. 'Come. Smell this,'
and he held the tin of International Roast instant coffee
under my nose.

I breathed it in. It smelt like coffee. I was used to making
it for Mum in the mornings and then after that she had
tea for the rest of the day.

'Now,' he said, 'smell this!'

He picked up a knife and slit open the shiny red square
packet that was on the bench. I could smell it even before

he brought it near, something rich and earthy and strong. It filled my head, filled the room. It sent me spinning.

'*This* is coffee!' he said.

Mum was smiling now, pouring hot water into her cup, putting in her artificial sweeteners, click, click.

'This is coffee,' Bo said again as he heaped a big spoonful into the filter paper that was folded carefully into the lid of his black thermos. He picked up the kettle and poured the water in very slowly.

'I'll be finished mine by the time yours is ready,' Mum said.

With that he put the kettle down and grabbed her cup and tipped the contents down the sink. Mum started to laugh. She held on to Bo and she looked small there against him. He put his arm around her, leant his head down to the side so that it was resting on hers.

'You don't even have a whisk,' he said.

THORNS IN MY SKIN

I fell on the cactus in our backyard.

My brother and I were playing cricket, just the two of us. I was bowling and he was batting and I went to catch the ball and I tripped backwards and landed on the big cactus in the corner of the garden.

My leg burned and when I looked there were hundreds of cactus thorns sticking into the flesh of my calf and my ankle. I tried to pull a few out with my fingertips, but the thorns were too small – too fine. They sunk down into my skin and were lost beneath the surface.

My brother ran over and said that my leg might turn black and drop off because cactus plants were poisonous. He said he saw that on a program on TV once. He helped me up the back stairs and we went inside. We sat on the couch and I tried to watch TV – tried to concentrate. My brother kept looking at my leg to see if it was going black. It wasn't, but it was red and swollen and it hurt a lot.

After about an hour we heard keys in the door, but it

wasn't Mum. It was Bo. He was carrying bags of shopping and when he walked into the lounge he told us that Mum was still at the library and he was going to make us dinner.

'She hurt her leg,' my brother said.

I sat in the bathroom on the edge of the bath.

It was the nicest room in the house, our bathroom. The warmest and brightest. It didn't really belong to the cottage because it was an extension, like the kitchen and the sunroom. It wasn't made of stone. Being in that bathroom was like being in someone else's house.

Bo brought the kettle, a yellow bucket and a box of camomile tea into the bathroom. He found the tea in the back of the kitchen cupboard. The box was dusty. There was a picture of white flowers on the front. Bo took the tea bags out of the box and tore them all open so that the tea was loose. It looked like chopped-up straw or chaff when it came out of the bags. It smelt like that too. Like horse feed or cow feed. Like wet lucerne.

'Whenever I had a splinter, my grandmother would soak my finger in camomile tea,' he said. 'It draws out the splinter.'

When the hot liquid cooled enough he told me to put my leg in the bucket. He asked if it was okay and I said yes. The warm water felt good against my skin.

'There are so many little accidents on the ship,' he said. 'I am good at fixing people up.'

Bo stayed with me in the bathroom. He sat on the bench

next to the sink and the sun was coming in through the window and in through the skylight and all the wood panelling held the warmth. I almost felt sleepy then. I wanted to close my eyes.

Bo started talking about his home, when he was young, about how the summers were bright and long, and even though there was plenty of light to go around, he never wanted to sleep. He never wanted to miss a minute of the sun.

'I would make myself stay awake in the night and in the day,' he said. 'I wanted to take in the light. But I could not last without sleep. I would go down to one of the little bays near my house. I would go down and lie on the sand or take out our small wooden rowboat that was on the shore. Those little bays were so calm – calm and sunny and bright – that I would fall asleep not meaning to. I would just fall asleep, dreaming about the light.' Bo smiled then. 'It was my home.'

I tried to imagine this place in my mind, a small island that was light for the whole of summer, and I knew I would like that very much. To be in the light. I would like that.

The mixture in the bucket was almost cold and Bo told me that I could take my leg out. He said that it had been in for long enough and he knelt down on the floor. He handed me a towel and I carefully wiped my leg. He was so tall and he had to crouch down even when I lifted my leg

right up. He took every thorn out one by one with Mum's tweezers. He did it very slowly and carefully. Some of the spines drew blood when they came up. I tried not to look.

When he got to the end of my leg, he held my foot up and touched the scar near my ankle. It was jagged and white and it made the flesh of my leg dimple in where it drew the skin tight together.

'Where did you get this?' he asked.

'I had an accident,' I said.

He nodded. He didn't ask me any more about it. He didn't ask me and I did not tell him about how Dad would sit me on the petrol tank of his motorbike and how one time, when we were going up to the very back of the farm, I slipped down and my leg got stuck in some part of the bike – some moving part that I couldn't see. But I could feel it, my skin ripping. I screamed out for Dad to stop, but he couldn't hear me, or at least he didn't stop, not until we got there, up the hill to the back of the farm. By then there was a ring of flesh scraped from my calf and blood seeping into my shoe.

Dad told me not to tell Mum I'd done it on the bike. He told me to just tell her that I caught my leg on the fence or tripped up on the gravel. I don't remember getting home to the dark brick-veneer farmhouse, but when Mum got home with my brother my leg was bandaged and I never even had to lie because Dad said, 'She hurt her leg but it's all fine now.' Mum never even looked at the bandage. She just walked into the kitchen and started cooking dinner.

* * *

'Imagine the scar is a picture that you like,' Bo said. 'Like a tattoo. Any picture. It has been drawn on your leg and only you can see it. Only you can imagine what the picture is.'

I looked for a long time, and I tried hard not to cry, because I couldn't see any picture there. I couldn't see anything.

'It must have hurt very much', Bo said.

'Yes,' I said.

When my leg was better, Bo said, 'Shall we kill the cactus?' He had a big knife, one of his sharp knives from the ship.

We walked down the back steps to the garden.

'You go first,' he said, and he offered me the knife, but I didn't take it.

With one swipe, he cut the cactus in half. Then in half again, and again.

He killed the cactus, cut it up into little pieces. And later, when he had gone, I hacked into the earth with the pointy end of one of the cricket stumps and made sure that every root, every fibre of that cactus was gone so it would never grow back again.

BIRDS CALL DOWN
THE MORNING

Birds call down the morning
 I feel it lift off me, the weight of darkness
 It is a new day.

'The light gets more every day,' Bo said.

I looked out from the sunroom to the purple sky, and it was such a relief to see it – the light. The day coming.

I sat close to Bo, at the table, without touching. I wanted to tell him that I was afraid of the darkness. I wanted to tell him but I stayed silent.

We were still.

'Yes, the light comes more and more every day,' he said again. 'A minute in the morning – a minute in the night.'

Minutes of time, two minutes a day.

Two minutes and two minutes and two minutes, until the birds start to sing at four a.m. and I wake with them.

I thought about before, my brother and me in that small attic room. Sometimes I could not tell if I was asleep or I was awake but we would be there in the dark and my brother would ask me if it was morning or night. I could not tell, and I was not brave enough to move, to get up and look behind the thick curtains. It was always so cold, the air, the room. The night pressing down on us both.

I would wait and listen, wait to see if I could hear birds in the garden. I would strain to hear them in the silence, and finally they would come – a soft call. A wave would wash over me. *It's all right now – the morning is coming. We are safe.*

My brother and I would get up, get out of that small attic room, and we would put on lots of clothes to keep warm and go down to the kitchen. We'd sit at the round green wooden table that was like my grandmother's but was not my grandmother's.

We would wait for Mum to wake up.

Bo's eyes turned to me, but I could not look at them. I could not show him all the fear that was there inside of me. So I kept looking out the window, at the morning, at the day. And he started to talk. He started to tell me about the sea.

'As we move south on the water, I lose track of the sunrise. At first I say, *Yes! I will watch every sunrise. Every one.* Then after five days, ten days, depending on the speed we are travelling and how far south we have come, the sun pops up when I am not ready. I wake at three a.m. and it

is already there. I feel cheated then. I feel lazy and think, *How have I let myself miss it?*

'But after weeks, time starts to go completely. We are just working, *Nella* going on and on. Sometimes the sun is always there. Sometimes it goes down for a small rest, a few hours. The days at sea become one giant day. There are just tasks. Simple tasks. Sleep. Make coffee. Wash the roasting pans. Refill the sugar. Defrost the lamb. Cook the soup. Make the eggs – fried, poached, scrambled. Then sleep and then tasks. Sleep, then tasks.

'My mind stops always thinking, stops worrying. Then I just am. I am just there. I am just a man. Working. Part of the ship. This kind of family. I do not have time to worry.'

I looked at Bo then, his face calm, talking about his life at sea. I looked at his eyes, grey and blue with movement like the water was there inside of them.

All the things he told me, I wanted more than anything.

LIKE SUNSHINE

My brother watched Leo.

Watched the large hands covered in flour stretch out the sticky pastry in long, thin strips. Leo shaped it, made small rounds and filled them with custard. He made larger pastries too, ones that were shaped in loops that folded around each other. Then he piped in the custard, so fast and with such precision, and I could smell the sweet almond smell – the custard shiny and yellow with egg yolks.

When I looked up at the tall man, at Leo, he was on autopilot. He could have had his eyes closed, because his hands knew the way. They were independent from him somehow, working steadily – loop and loop and loop and cut. Loop and loop and loop and cut.

When they were finished, the pastries were like crowns, emblems of power. Sweet dough loops of magic. Almond flakes, marzipan, more custard, egg wash.

Leo took the full tray and slotted it in the oven near the top. I could feel the heat on my face all the way from

across the galley. He took another tray out, a hot tray – the pastries on it all golden and sun-kissed, the custard bubbling. He set it down on the stainless-steel bench, looked at my brother and winked.

'Now we taste!' he said.

My brother's face burst open into a smile. He moved closer to the bench, a few steps, but I stayed where I was. I watched Leo cut two pastries in half. The custard inside moved like lava – slow and thick – and it pooled on the tray. Leo put two halves on a small plate, pushed it towards us. I knew my brother was staring at the plate and that his small hands were holding on to the edge of the bench, but I kept my eyes on Leo. I watched his face, saw the way he looked down at the pastries – his work. Content. He breathed in, picked up one of the cut halves and took a bite.

Leo's eyes closed then. He chewed and chewed then swallowed. He wiped his mouth with his hand and said a word, just quietly – a word I didn't know, a Danish word, *sólskin*, and when he opened his eyes he was looking right at me.

'Sunshine,' he said, 'like sunshine.'

My brother looked at me, his hand already reaching out for the plate. I moved closer.

That first bite. Crisp buttery flakes, sweet warm custard oozing – sharp marzipan and almond. The eggs, the sugar, the crunch of pastry – made with big hands. Made with

skill and care. Made for breakfast – to start the day – to greet the sun. A magic loop of pastry.

The light coming through the porthole made the whole galley fill with yellow. I breathed it in.

A BAG OF MIXED LOLLIES

The wind started to blow ice when I was halfway home from the shop. I hadn't noticed the streets until then, until the cold wind made my face raw. All I could think about was the white paper bag of mixed lollies I had in my hand.

They were for my brother.

He'd just sat there on the floor in his school uniform, one grey sock pulled up to his knee, the other scrunched down around his ankle, when Mum came in and burst into tears and told us about Tom Balinski. About how he had been hit by a car on the way home from school.

About how he was dead.

He didn't cry, my brother. I didn't see him cry. I only saw his body shake – just a shudder, like something very small had collapsed inside his bones.

The accident was on the news. Flashing lights reflecting off a fallen schoolbag, the emblem of a waratah with the Latin words that meant *No Man is an Island* shining out in the dark. The man on the TV got it wrong, because he

said it was a high school boy who had been hit by a car and died from his injuries on the way to the hospital. But it wasn't a high school boy. It was a small boy.

A boy just as small as my brother.

Tom had come to my brother's birthday party three days before. He was like an angel with his white hair and blue eyes – his skin so pale. Not see-through like mine, just creamy and pale. He gave my brother a really huge pencil case. It was all the bright colours in stripes and I knew my brother really liked it because he carried it around with him for a long time after the party, after everyone had gone. And he carefully put all of his pencils and pens inside and put it in his schoolbag ready for school the next day. Monday. Then there was Tuesday and then there was Wednesday.

The day Tom Balinski died.

I was on the bus and I had seen Tom and my brother walking out of the school gate together. My brother got on the bus and he waved to Tom and Tom waved back – his hair bright against the grey sky and the grey of his uniform. I remember that it started to rain as the bus pulled away.

When I got back from the shop my brother was on the couch. He was in his pyjamas and the doona from his bed was over his legs. Molly, our cat, was sitting on him, but when I came close she jumped off and ran away. Molly didn't like me very much.

I told my brother that I got him some lollies and I held out the bag. I must have been twisting it over and over on the way home because the paper at the top was all grimy and creased and torn. My brother took the bag in his hand. He held it for a while and then he put it down next to him on the couch. I told him there were no liquorice things.

'Thanks,' he said.

The next day at school, my teacher, Mr Peters, said that we didn't have to do the usual timetable and that we could work on anything we wanted. He asked if we would like him to read to us, and we all said yes. It was the best part of the day when Mr Peters read. He was reading a book that he had written and it was about some kids who had found a portal through time. I don't remember what it was called or the names of the characters now, but I remember that I was captivated by it then.

I listened to the story – to the words spoken in Mr Peters' soft, low, rolling voice. I looked out of the window and I watched the sky, watched the clouds moving. I saw my brother's class walk out across the lawn, all of them. The whole class. Most of them were holding hands.

Their teacher was Mrs Davison and she was tall and had long blonde hair and she was very beautiful, I thought. I knew that my brother really loved her. I think all of her students loved her. She looked like a shepherd among her flock. She was like a shepherd – the children gathered

around her, gathered close, under one of the old chestnut trees where kids played conkers at recess. And they all sat down. Mrs Davison had papers in her hands.

Mr Peters stopped reading. He put the book away but I kept looking out of the window. Even when other kids were busy working on projects, I just sat and looked out of the window. And my brother's class stayed out there under that old chestnut tree all day. They had lunch together, and in the late afternoon they walked back to their classroom with Mrs Davison leading the way.

They were all still holding hands.

HIS NAME WAS TOM

The Priest called him Tomas, but my brother called him Tom. He was Tom, and they shared a language that was silent to everyone else but them. I would hear them laughing from my room. Little giggles, little stories about things I would never know.

The coffin was small and white and people stood up one by one and laid flowers on top. There were so many flowers that some fell to the floor and were left behind when the coffin was carried out of the church.

My brother sat still and Mum cried and I could feel the cold from the stones below my feet move up my legs. My body was going to sleep – becoming stone like the floor, like the walls. The darkness was getting in.

After the ceremony, my brother stood with some other boys from his class and Tom's mother talked to them. I couldn't hear the words, but her eyes were soft. They seemed to be filled with peace – some kind of love. She touched my brother's curly hair with her hand and smiled.

Then she bent down and grabbed him up tightly in her arms. She held him close, my brother's body limp and stiff. Her mouth was moving like she was singing in my brother's ear. Like she was praying. It seemed to go on for a long time. And my brother's body softened, his arms reached up and wrapped around her. He hugged her back.

When she let my brother go, her face was puffy, her eyes half-closed. She stood up tall and touched my brother's hair one more time, then she turned and walked away.

Mum put us in the car and told us she wouldn't be long. We were in our school uniforms and were meant to go back to school for the afternoon, but I hoped we didn't have to go. It was getting late and it didn't seem right that my brother should have to go to school today.

Well-dressed people in suits and in dresses and hats walked to their cars. I saw the principal of our new school go past. She had a beehive hair-do. She always wore it up like that – in a beehive, like my grandmother did.

'I just feel bad for her,' my brother said.

'Who?' I asked, but he didn't answer. He sat there looking down. The bells of the church rang out in a chord – a simple harmony, over and over.

'I hope we don't have to go back to school,' I said.

My brother shrugged. I saw Mum come out of the church. She wiped her nose on a white tissue then stuffed it back up the sleeve of her cardigan. She always had a tissue up her sleeve in case she needed one.

'I just feel bad for her,' my brother said again, and he looked right at me – right in my eyes. 'We're not dead but Tom is and she won't ever see him again.'

The bells of the church kept on ringing.

SNOW DAY

A week after the funeral it snowed. I could smell it before I even opened my eyes. Snow, thick and solid in the window box. So much of it that it covered half my bedroom window.

It was really there.

It had begun to fall softly in the darkness the night before, just as bedtime loomed, and Mum told us that it wouldn't last.

'It will melt away and be gone by morning,' she said. 'It's nearly summer!'

And it was nearly summer. It was November. A school night.

We stood together on the back deck and felt the snow melt on our skin and dampen our hair. It was so silent. A blanket of silence.

I lay in my bed in the dark and listened. Listened to see if I could hear it falling out there in the night, covering over our car and filling all the stone gutters, dusting the red

roses powdery white. I fell asleep trying to listen – willing the snow to fall harder so it would cover up all of the greyness of this place. Until it made these old streets white and clean and new.

School was cancelled.

We played out in the street all day with kids we didn't know, kids we had never even met, and West Hobart never looked so good. So bright.

A man skied down Hill Street. I watched him disappear and I hoped he knew how to stop. There were no cars, no buses. Nothing but kids screaming and running and skidding over, throwing snowballs and hoping that the snow would stay for weeks and weeks.

By that night it was just slush, muddied up and used. And in the morning there were only little pockets of frosted snow left in the deep round gutters, wherever the sun didn't shine.

The magic was gone.

We drove to school the next day wearing our grey uniforms that offered no warmth and my brother was quiet again. Quiet and lost somewhere trying not to think about things.

I could not help him.

MS *Nella Dan*
Voyage 2, 1986/1987 Season
10th November 1986
Position: 63° 52.000' S, 119° 55.000' E
Captain's note: Vessel moving through leads in pack ice.
Occasional small icebergs. Strong winds expected by 14.00.

We feel *Nella* butt up against the ice, that first big jolt, and
Soren calls out, 'Mooooose! Mooooose!'

Erik answers the call. He runs at Soren, leaps in the air,
and their chests smack together in the usual ritual. *Thud.*
Thud. 'Mooooose!'

I'm scrubbing pans, the lunch shift over. Our one hour
a day off. *Nella* lifts up, slides over the ice with a squeal.
The pressure of the ship on the ice forms waves underneath
and they roll and buck and lash out. We pitch like we are
on open water, then steady up – move ahead. Steady. Five
knots, slow and steady.

'Time for coffee,' Soren says, and I say, 'Okay,' dry
my hands, last pan done. I get out our special thermos –
chipped and marked and dented on the bottom from being

dropped so many times. I open the lid.

Soren tells me that we better get that side of beef out from the freezer before we forget and I nod. I look at him. Both our arms come up at the same time. *One, two, three* – rock, paper, scissors.

Soren always chooses rock first. Every time. I don't know why, but it makes it easy to beat him. I go paper. He stands there looking at my open hand. Paper.

'Best of three?' he says. It is what he *always* says. I nod. I give him a chance.

One, two, three.

This time *he* goes paper. I go scissors. It just popped into my head at the very last second. Scissors. Two fingers. He shakes his head, always so defeated, starts walking towards the metal stairs. Then he stops, turns to me.

'I let you win,' he says.

'Sure,' I say. 'Sure.'

I take a scoop of ground coffee. The smell of it fills my head, my stomach, and I am looking forward to it – fresh coffee. Maybe I will sit in the red booth and read the printed news from home. Maybe I will just stare out at the ice, at the world there moving right by us.

I see Soren start to go down the stairs to the coolroom. *Nella* slows, her little frame is humming, pushing against the thick ice. Then she lurches forward, rides right over to the port side heavy. I brace against the bench. The pile of pans I washed fall to the floor. The thermos tips, coffee grounds spill all over the stainless steel. I hear crashing

from the mess, broken plates, smashing glass, God knows what breaking.

I feel *Nella* right herself, pull back – her engine revving. I move to the stairwell.

'Soren?' I say.

A foot.

A leg.

A man on his stomach in the small space between the bottom of the metal stairs and the coolroom doors. Arms out in front of him, head twisted to one side.

I open my mouth, call his name. I scream for help and the sound echoes down the stairs. I look at my hands, shaking and coffee-stained. *Nella* just keeps on slicing and shuddering through the ice. She just keeps on moving.

I run down the stairs, take Soren's wrist in my hand. It's warm, his skin still warm, but I can find no pulse. His eyes are open. They stare at the wall.

I hear shouting, footsteps on the metal stairs. I see faces, serious faces. I am pulled up and out of the way. I lean against the coolroom doors. There is blood on my shoe, blood on my trousers. I must have been kneeling in it.

There on the floor, a pool of blood.

The master is opposite me. We are sitting in the red booth. I don't remember getting here. I don't know how long I have been sitting here for.

'There is nothing we can do,' he says. 'He has passed.'

I nod. I look at nothing.

'Why don't you go, get cleaned up?' he says, but I tell him I want to stay.

We sit there.

'Just a terrible accident,' he says. 'Terrible.'

There's a body bag brought down from somewhere. Crew keep coming into the galley, hearing the news. No one can believe it. It's not real. It can't be right.

Klaus comes over.

'Dinner is off,' he says. 'I'll put out soup, some sandwiches.'

'Yes,' I say, 'the soup's ready,' thinking about the cauliflower soup I made after breakfast.

He pats me on the shoulder then, something he has never done. Like a father would. Like a brother.

We wrap Soren up and take him into the freezer. No one says a word. I keep thinking he will just wake up, say, 'Got you! That was a good one.' But when the captain closes Soren's eyes with the weight of his fingers, something inside me goes very cold.

Someone hands me a glass of whisky and I drink it down. Then another. Another. That night we sat in the passage – riding out the storm – he said to me, 'I know I'm meant to be here, on this ship.'

We drank to that. To all his plans. Antarctica and all that we would see. To the bar he would open, to all of the adventures that would be his.

'Here's to us,' he said, and we drank down our whisky, which tasted bitter to me, but I was going along for the ride. Being part of it. That feeling. He made you feel like freedom.

'Lucky,' he said. 'You and me. Christ!'

I sit in my cabin in clean clothes. I don't know where the ones I was wearing are. Outside the ice is getting tough – sticking together in sheets, in rounds.

If I'd just let him win rock, paper, scissors, then I would be drinking my coffee, reading the news from home, and Soren would be bugging me – talking nonstop the way he always did, asking me about this and about that. Talking about his camera, about the photos he took yesterday, about the ones he's going to take tomorrow. Talking about the Rolling Stones. About Pink Floyd. About the stars and the gods and about everything that's in that head of his. And I know from now on that the silence of Soren not talking will be terrifying. That it will be the loneliest sound of all.

MS *Nella Dan*

Voyage 2, 1986/1987 Season

11th November 1986

Position: 63° 26.000' S, 120° 5.000' E

Captain's note: Pack ice in all directions. Icebergs in the distance. We continue at slow speed.

The captain puts down a cup of coffee for me, black, and I take it.

'I know you were close,' he says.

I tell him what happened. I tell him everything – the frozen beef and the coffee break and the ship pitching up over the ice.

We sit like that – I sip my coffee and so does he. Up here it is much quieter than below, the engine sounds muted. Up here, high in the sky, there is no smell of diesel fuel or roasting meats. No smell of cabbage. The porthole is slightly open and it's nice to have air – cold and clean and alive.

'I'm very sorry,' he says.

I nod. The moments pass. I finish my coffee.

'I knew your father, you know,' he says. 'I was young, just a deck boy then.'

I look at him. His long hair is slicked back, his face calm. I think of my father sitting out in the sunlight at home, smoking his pipe. His eyes closed, his face at peace – classical music playing on the radio, his mind far away, somewhere that I could never reach. His mind always at sea.

'Sometimes I feel like I hardly knew him,' I say. I stare at the bulkhead, then at the floor. 'He took me on this ship when she was launched. I was only two, I think. We sailed down from Aalborg to Copenhagen. I don't really remember, but it happened. I have the photograph. My grandmother came. She got very sick, even in the harbour.'

I smile then. I start to smile. 'She was not made of the sea.' I meant to say 'for the sea' but then 'of' seems right so I leave the word there. I leave it.

'Do you need to call anyone?' he asks. 'Call home?'

I sit for a second. I try to think.

'I don't need to call,' I say.

'Okay,' he says, and he finishes his coffee. He puts his cup down on the desk. I stand up. 'Thank you,' I say. He shakes my hand, puts his other hand over it tightly.

'I want the galley crew to take tonight off, and just a light breakfast in the morning. Tomorrow is a day of rest, must-do duties only. Come and see me anytime.'

I nod, my head light, my eyes blinking. I walk out of the office and down the passage. I walk down the stairs and down another passage on the deck where the expeditioners

sleep, one hand on the bulkhead, the other hand clutching my stomach. I open the heavy door to outside and the cold air rushes at my face. I step out into the blinding light.

There are islands of white going on and on for as far as I can see, the water almost black in between, but over the side where *Nella* slowly cuts her way through the ice, the water is churned up turquoise blue.

Steady, steady, we move at half-speed, and when I look up, a cape petrel is just above me, flying with us. Little turns, little wings. I reach my arm up, my fingers stretch. I reach and for a second the bird comes so close I can almost touch him. I can see his eyes, his tiny face. He looks at me, then rises up with the thermals. Up and up at full speed until I lose him in the light.

My eyes are full.

* * *

Where does the land end and the sea begin?

He asked me this question once at our little beach.

I was very small, I don't know how old, but I remember I ran down to the water, drew a line in the sand with my finger and said, 'Here, Papa! Here.'

My father smiled and nodded and we kept on walking together in silence. He liked to walk when he was home from sea. To walk in a straight line and to keep on going and not be stopped by anything. We would often walk for hours, it seemed, along tracks and through fields and down

small lanes, me just a step behind. Me trying to keep up with his big legs.

I follow you.

When we got back to our beach, my line was gone – swallowed up by the tide. Everything was different, the landscape changed.

My father turned to me and said, 'The sea is alive and there is no beginning and there is no end. It moves with the moon and with the spinning of this earth and it calls us when it wants us to come.'

That night I lay in my bed, I pulled the covers over me tight, and in the darkness I said over and over in my head, *Don't call me. Don't call me, because I don't want to go.*

MS *Nella Dan*
Voyage 2, 1986/1987 Season
12th November 1986
Position: 63° 26.000' S, 120° 5.000' E
Captain's note: We have spent the past 6 hours in heavy ice covered in a deep layer of snow. There is no open water in sight of the vessel, just frozen leads. First officer is at the helm, but we have been unable to move more than a few metres in any direction.

I wake to see Erik's face, blurred, above me. A pain in the side of my head.

'Bo?' he says. 'Bo, it's eight a.m.'

I jump up. I can feel the emptiness of my stomach.

'We're stuck,' he says and he points to the porthole.

I can't register what he is saying. I squint, focus. Outside, a landscape of white – only white. We are not moving.

'I have to get back,' he says. 'The expeditioners are hungry.'

I stand there, afraid. How had I not woken? I always wake when the engine sound changes. All of us do. Always.

The engine sounds are the best sleeping pill. The constant sound of them cuts out all other sounds. The sound of

everything is fine. You are safe. You can sleep. But even if we just slow down, or speed up a tiny bit, if the engine noise changes, I wake.

Last night I had slept like the dead.

I had been dead.

And we are stuck.

everything is fine. You are safe. You can steer, but even
if we just slow down, or speed up a tiny bit, if the engine
noise changes, I wake.

Last night I had slept like the dead.

I had been dead.

And we are stuck.

MS *Nella Dan*
Voyage 2, 1986/1987 Season
18th December 1986
Position: 63° 26.000' S, 120° 5.000' E
Captain's note: Vessel surrounded by ice. Dense pack ice in
all directions. Icebergs in the distance.

Four weeks. Five weeks.

We are still stuck.

The work goes on.

There is food – plenty of food. It would take many
months to run out, but the fresh vegetables are going. Now
we are making salad with grated carrot and lemon juice.
Just carrot. No one wants to eat it.

Twelve weeks since we left Hobart. A lifetime.

The winterers have already been so long without fresh
fruit, fresh vegetables. They ask me if there are any bananas.
They ask with such hope.

'No,' I say. 'I'm sorry.'

I ask them if there is something I can make them,
anything special, but they shake their heads.

'I just can't stop thinking about bananas.'

In the store, cabbage, grapefruit, cauliflower, carrots, potatoes. In the coolroom, enough meat and supplies to last.

In the freezer, a body bag that we must pass every day.

Somehow we have run out of onions.

I sit on my bunk, blink against the light flooding in through my small, round porthole. The sun is relentless. It won't leave me alone – won't let me rest. The night, it never comes.

Work goes on – breakfast, lunch, dinner – only we are one man down, one man gone. Today, at lunch, I put the palm of my hand against the hotplate.

Klaus grabbed me, shook me hard.

'Are you mad?' he yelled, but then he softened. He sent me to the doctor and then to my cabin, my hand bandaged. He told me to rest.

I don't know why I did it. Maybe to see if I could feel something. I don't know. I wasn't really there.

The sun shines down outside. The sun is God.

I see movement, shadows. I stand closer to the glass and out the porthole small figures move on the ice. Men dressed in snow gear, blue, yellow, arms waving, legs running. A black-and-white ball in the air, flying.

A game of football.

I pick up the camera off my desk – Soren's camera. I wonder what's on the roll of film inside. What photos did he take? I aim the lens at the porthole, look through

the viewfinder. A perfect circle of light against the black inside my cabin. I take the shot.

Such a strange thing to see. A game of football on the ice. A game of football by the side of a red ship in the middle of the frozen ocean.

I put the camera back down on my desk. I look at my bandaged hand. I have this urge to run. I put on my snow boots, my warm jacket and gloves. I get out of my cabin and walk down the passage, go up and outside to the ladder on the cargo hold. I step down backwards – down, down the rungs, down to the thick ice that holds us. Metres and metres of hard frozen water.

I move towards the game, towards the grunting and screaming. Towards the laughing. My breath is puffs of white vapour, the air cold on my face. A few of the crew are playing. I see the second mate, Carsten, and he waves me over.

I start to run.

My feet move and I keep on running. I chase the ball until there is sweat down my back – sweat on my face. I miss a shot and slip over, slide on the ice. The ball skids out away from me, but I get to my feet fast and make it to the ball before anyone else. I kick hard towards the goal – a solid shot. A lucky strike.

Someone grabs me from behind, yells out, 'GOAL!' They try to lift me up but we both fall over hard, crunching into the wet ice.

'Christ!' they say, and for a second I think it's Soren. Soren saying, 'Christ!' the way he did. Soren laughing like

a madman with that spark in his blue eyes. But the light lessens and the face in front of me becomes clear. Grey eyes, round face. It's Carsten.

'Goal!' he says again. 'Victory!' He pumps his arm in the air and helps me to my feet.

'The Danes will not be beaten,' he says.

There are only three of us, and anyway, no one is keeping score, but it feels good to kick a goal, feel my heart beat hard, my blood pump, have my lungs pull cold air in with ease. To play this game.

We run until we are hollow, slip and skid over until our pants are sodden. We run until we are nearly sick and can no longer breathe.

The wonder of this place hits me with full force. The ice – the sun high in a blue sky – night and day. I'm here on the ice, here in this wonderland.

Lucky. And I want to be alive.

We climb up the ladder, one by one, unified by a small black-and-white ball. A team. We have beaten the frustration of being stuck for one day. One good day.

I tell the others I will go and organise brandy and some hot chocolate. I find Klaus in the galley and tell him I am fine, that I can come and work, but he shakes his head. He tells me dinner is prepared and I should go and have a drink, take the day, the evening, the night.

'Take the day,' he says. He winks at me but his voice is stern. It is an order.

I go up and sit in the passenger lounge, a place I have

never been before. We pass a bottle of brandy around, drink out of coffee cups. A bottle of whisky, a bottle of vodka, a bottle of cognac. I don't know where all the bottles came from. Someone has a bottle of port but I don't have any of that. Too sweet. Too sickly. I stay well clear.

I go down to the toilet and on the way back decide to get some beers. A small gift on my part. No one is down in our bar, the Frozen Inn, still too early. I write it up in the book – *Bo, 24 Carlsberg.*

We are almost out of beer. We will run out tomorrow or the next day. I will enjoy these last beers. I will make the most of them.

When I carry the green bottles up the stairs in a crate, everyone is grateful. The cold beer goes down so well. One of the scientists says, 'Thank God it isn't the akvavit, we would be dead from that!'

It is true. I have seen passengers unable to walk after a few glasses. They seem fine, but then they can't get up off their chairs. Their legs have stopped working.

The sun is still up high with us – up high in the air in the passenger lounge.

A man called John pulls out a guitar, and he's good – knows how to play. His long, thin fingers strum strongly and he has a nice voice. I only know some of the songs, but people start to sing along with the choruses, loudly, out of tune, and it's impossible not to join in. 'We Are the Champions', 'You Can't Always Get What You Want', 'Hey Jude', 'Go Your Own Way'.

'Father and Son'.

The first notes of that song make everyone stand up. We hold on to each other's shoulders in a round, sing together. We sing with all our hearts, a family – Cat Stevens. 'Father and Son'.

I feel like a boy again, my first years at sea. The wonder and hope and the boredom of long days. Laughing at the hard work. Laughing at the big seas. Being out in the world and saying, come on, I will take it all and more. Missing home but thinking ahead and not behind. Keeping my eyes on the horizon.

The song ends, and we are puffed. John puts down his guitar and some of us climb out onto the monkey deck. Someone hands out cigars and I take one. It feels like as good a time as any to try my first cigar. It is rough and warm and I smoke it with gusto – my arm around John's neck, like we are the oldest friends in the world. He yells out, 'Goddamn you, ice!' and we all start chanting, 'Let us free! Let us free! Let us free!' our feet stomping on the deck.

The bald head of Jens the chief engineer appears at the top of the ladder. He tells us that it is all good and well that we are asking the gods to let us free, but he thinks for now everyone needs to come inside and eat some dinner.

'And, by the way, your captain is trying to sleep below your feet, if you don't mind!'

He turns to leave, but catches my eye.

'Bo. God. I didn't see you there. Okay for some.'

It's late, ten p.m. The sun deceptively high. Sunburn

on the expeditioners' cheeks and probably on mine too.
Our stomachs full of whisky and brandy and beer and not
crying out yet for food.

John turns to me, his eyes strained and red.

'My wife is having a baby any day, and I'm stuck here,
bloody useless.'

'That's tough,' I say.

He shakes his head. 'I'm going to bloody start digging us
out tomorrow. I'm going to get a shovel and bloody dig us out.'

Down in the mess, we eat like we haven't eaten for days.
The food tastes so good – the warm salty gravy and the
crisp roast pork, the acid of the cabbage all going down
together well.

I wash up our dishes and put the leftover food away.
I feel the need to go and lie down. My feet heavy, my eyes
half-closed – suddenly drunk and only thinking of bed.

I fall into my bunk, kick my boots off to the floor. Four
a.m. tomorrow morning will be the start of a new working
day. I will be myself again. But today, I had been someone
else. A passenger. A boy. I had been free. Something hard
and heavy had fallen away – crumbled, turned to dust out
there on the football field.

Sleep.

Sleep.

Let me sleep.

MS *Nella Dan*
Voyage 2, 1986/1987 Season
27th December 1986
Position: 63° 26.000′ S, 120° 5.000′ E
Captain's note: Vessel surrounded by ice. Japanese ice breaker, *Maru Shirase*, arrived after breakfast. They will attempt to tow us to a clear lead.

They gave us a bag of apples. They broke us out of the ice.

I waved goodbye to them on their huge ship, the *Maru Shirase*. They even had a tennis court on the aft deck. *A tennis court.*

I bite into an apple – cold, crisp – and the sound of my teeth sinking through the skin makes the hair on the back of my neck stand up. My mouth fills with the sweet liquid – so familiar. I chew and chew, my eyes closed.

Just an apple – an apple.

But I have never tasted anything so necessary to me.

Apples, always there on the trees and in the cupboard. Apple in so much of the food I love. I won't forget this now.

Seven weeks without one, and out of everything missing,

out of everything gone, this is what I've missed, what I thought about, the most.

The cold, crisp taste of an apple. My teeth sinking through the skin.

MS *Nella Dan*
Voyage 2, 1986/1987 Season
8th January 1987
Position: 45° 8.000' S, 142° 33.000' E
Captain's note: We continue on schedule for our arrival in
Hobart at 09.00 tomorrow.

His cabin door remains open.

I pass it six times a day, maybe more, but I never look in. I look ahead – eyes straight ahead. I pass by quickly. But tonight, I stop at his door. I don't know why. I don't know, but I stand there. I look inside.

My eyes grow accustomed to the light and outlines become solid. Soren's system of mess. His clothes, his boots, his books and magazines all over the floor. His bed unmade, the duvet hanging off the side.

He always said that he didn't need to clean up because he knew where everything was and if he moved things, he wouldn't be able to find anything. On the way from Denmark, somewhere near the equator on the Indian Ocean, Klaus told him to clean up his *stinking* cabin. We

had only been gone for about three weeks. But Soren said that it wasn't a mess. He said it was a system.

'I know where everything is. If I need a pen I know exactly where one will be.' And he picked up a pair of trousers that were in a ball on the floor and there, underneath, was a pen.

'See!' he said.

Klaus shook his head and told him to clean up, but he was smiling, maybe even laughing about the pen. It was impossible to stay mad at Soren.

I step inside. I sit on his bunk.

His survival bag is by my feet, open with some of the contents spilling out. It makes me smile because it should be in the cupboard, tightly closed – *In Case of an Emergency*. We have to take it with us to drills, when we stand outside on the helideck, freezing, smoking cigarettes and waiting for our names to be called so we can go back inside.

Opposite me, on the built-in desk, secured by towels rolled up and jammed in on either side, is the CD player he had bought in Hobart. Black and shiny and new – AKAI written in silver.

'You have to come and listen! Listen to the quality!' Soren would say.

We'd squeeze in. He'd put on 'Money for Nothing' by Dire Straits and we would stand and listen.

'Doesn't it sound amazing? So much better than tapes!'

With the constant grind of the engines and the ocean smacking the hull, we could not really hear the difference. We were just being polite, I guess, or just happy to listen to music together. Happy to be crammed in a cabin that wasn't our own. A change of scenery from the Frozen Inn or from our own tiny cabins. A different song. A different space. Something new.

But Soren only had two CDs. *The Wall* and *Brothers in Arms*.

I lean over and press the power button. There is a bass sound that I feel in my chest and the red light comes on. Then a song starts up, loud and getting louder. I grab the headphones that are on the floor and plug them in. I pull them over my ears. I close down the outside world.

I listen. I lie back on Soren's bunk and close my eyes. It's so loud, it almost hurts, but I don't want to turn it down.

Blasts of full colour, details bright and bursting. A whole orchestra, a choir, a band, all there in the headphones – all there in my head. Inside of me – sounds I have heard but never felt and I am lost, floating high on this giant wave. The words reaching into me. The words. Pink Floyd – 'Comfortably Numb'.

* * *

'It's the new thing,' he said. 'The sound. The real business!'

I looked at the stereo.

'It's so much money,' I said.

Soren gave me that look. 'What the hell are you saving for anyway?'

I shrugged. My house was old, needed a lot of fixing, but that's not what I said. I told him that maybe I'd like to stay here for a while. Stay for a bit.

'Travel?' he said.

I shrugged again. 'Maybe just stay here.'

Soren rolled his eyes then. I knew what he was thinking. There was a whole world of women out there and I hardly knew this woman, this place. It was too soon.

'I just have this good feeling,' I said, but he wasn't really listening. He was staring at the black shiny stereo that had this new sound inside of it.

We carried it out of the shop and all the way down to the wharf. He told me I could have his old stereo.

'It's better than your piece of shit,' he said.

I told him to give his to Erik and Jonas. They didn't have anything in their cabin. Anyway, I liked my old tape player. It never chewed up my tapes and it was good enough. It would do.

'Okay,' he said. 'You can stay in the past while the rest of us move into the future.'

I told him that he didn't have any CD things to put in this new machine. He laughed at that. But when we got to his cabin he was serious. He looked at me.

'Maybe you should take a chance,' he said. 'I guess sometimes you just have to say, fuck it! Life is short. I guess you could stay here for a bit – see how it goes.'

* * *

The last half of the song is just the thick bass, the lead guitar pulling the melody right out, lifting it up onto another level – the melody soaring to the horizon.

I let go of my body, of the ship, of this earth.

I can see for all of time.

'You were right, Soren,' I say. 'It's the real business.'

THE SNOWBALL

Bo and the crew threw snowballs at us when *Nella* came home. She had been stuck in ice for seven weeks. There was cheering and people were hugging and kissing. Some people were crying.

Everyone on board had missed Christmas. New Year's. January.

There was a news crew there. They filmed the snowballs, the celebration, and it was on the ABC news that night. The reporter said it was the longest besetment of modern times.

Bo saved one snowball for us. He put it in my brother's hand.

'Ice, all the way from Antarctica,' he said.

My brother told him about the day it snowed and how we got the day off school and made snowballs in the street and had a toboggan made from a tray, but it busted halfway down the hill.

Bo smiled, but on the way home in the car he stared out the window and was quiet. Mum told us that he had lost

his friend while they were away, that he had fallen down and hit his head very hard. He was a man who'd worked in the galley called Soren.

I remembered him. He was the man who lifted my brother up and gave him the box of chewing gum. I wanted to ask if they buried him in the ice, if they left him behind, but I didn't ask. I looked across at my brother. He had his eyes fixed on the snowball in his hand.

'Did you run out of food?' he said.

Bo didn't answer for a while, then, when he did, his voice was quiet. Faraway.

'We had enough food. We can last for a very long time. But we ran out of beer. And we ran out of apples. I missed them.'

My brother looked at me. He whispered, 'I wouldn't miss apples.'

Bo turned around in his seat.

'You would miss them if you didn't have them for so long. You would miss them,' he said.

My brother made his eyes wide, like he hadn't meant to say that, like it was something only meant for me. He went back to watching the snowball. It was shiny and had started to melt on the surface, but it was packed so tight and still so cold that it was not dripping yet. My brother had his jumper pulled down between it and his skin but his hand must have been getting very cold.

'If I put this in the freezer, do you think it will last?' he asked.

'Yes,' Bo said. 'Yes. We will put it in a plastic bag and put it in the freezer. It will last.'

As soon as we got home my brother ran into the kitchen and got a sandwich bag out from the drawer. He put the snowball in the bag and clipped it shut. Bo put it in the freezer for him.

'Anyway, don't worry. We leave again very soon and I can get you some more ice anytime. I can get you as much as you need.' Bo looked at him then. 'I missed your birthday,' he said.

My brother told him that he had a party and it was great, and Bo said he was sad to miss that.

'I will make you a cake. We can still have a cake even if it is late. We can have a cake for your birthday and a cake for the New Year.'

Mum told us to go and look at the *Women's Weekly Birthday Cake Book* and I knew that they wanted to be rid of us, so we sat in the dark lounge room, huddled on the floor, and I tried to listen to what Mum and Bo were talking about in the sunroom. I tried hard but I couldn't hear properly.

When my brother had narrowed the cake selection down to three possible choices, the ones with the most icing and lollies that he liked, Bo came in and said that he was going to try to sleep for a little while. He said he had not had much sleep for a long time and he suddenly looked very tired. I could see the hollows of his eye sockets, and his eyes

were not grey and they were not blue. They seemed to be no colour at all, like they had been washed out to nothing.

My brother said, 'Goodnight. See you in the morning,' even though it *was* morning. Even though it was only ten a.m.

'See you in the morning,' Bo said. Then he turned to me.

'You know what is a nice cake for the New Year? Chocolate-hazelnut-cherry cake.'

I had never even heard of a cake like that before, not ever, and I couldn't even imagine what it would be like.

THE CAKE

The cake was like a castle, a fortress – with turrets made of chocolate curls dusted with icing-sugar snow. There were layers of cake and between them were ground hazelnuts and cream and dark cherries that had come out of a can Bo got from the ship. He let me drink a bit of the juice that the cherries were in – it was sweet and rich and it stained my lips purple.

It took Bo a long time to make the cake. It seemed very complicated and there were lots of different parts to it. He didn't seem to mind how long it took. When the cake part was ready to go in the oven, Bo made himself a coffee and poured it into one of our glasses that was actually a small Vegemite jar. I don't know why he didn't use a cup – he must have liked the small glass, because he always used it when he was at our house.

'I miss coffee,' he said. 'The way it tastes at home.'

He took a sip, a taste, then held the small glass up to the light coming through the window.

'No matter how hard I try, it's not the same as at home. It should be the same – it's the same coffee and I make it the same. But it does not taste the same! This is some kind of problem. A mystery. Maybe it is the salt in the air, or because I am in the south, where everything is going backwards all the time. I don't know. It is some kind of mystery.'

Bo wouldn't let us watch him finish the cake. He told us it should be a surprise, so I went and watched TV with my brother until it was ready.

Bo carried the cake out to the sunroom. There was one candle already lit, burning bright, and it made the dusted icing glow and sparkle.

'Yes, I think this is my favourite type of cake,' he said when he put it down on the table. 'It's like being in the forest in the winter when the trees go to sleep, when the light isn't so bright and the river begins to freeze, then the snow is coming more and more, and everyone has their Christmas lights in the windows night and day, shining out, and you can smell spices in the air from all the special Christmas baking.'

And I could taste it – the dark rich earth of a forest filled with rabbits and deer, snow gently falling.

A fairytale.

TIME

Bo sat in the sunroom under the light.

I could see his back through the glass of the lounge-room door, his shoulders rounded in his white T-shirt. He didn't seem to feel the cold. He was smoking a cigarette. I watched him for a while – maybe it was for a long time, I don't know. It was the middle of the night and everyone was asleep. Everyone except for me and Bo.

I opened the door from the lounge to the sunroom. I walked in and stood at the table and Bo looked at me, his eyes dark.

'I can't sleep,' he said and he lit another cigarette.

He was leaving again in a few days. It was hardly any time – no time. Getting stuck in the ice had put everything out, the whole schedule for the summer. Everything was different now.

'No matter how long I sit here,' he said, 'I cannot decide. Should I send his watch home, or keep it safe here with me?'

I wasn't sure if he was asking me, and I didn't know the answer. I sat down quietly on the chair next to his.

The watch was on the table, an old-fashioned one, like the watch my grandpa wore. Only his was gold and a gift for twenty-five years of service at Smiths Industries, where he'd made clocks and watches and aeroplane black boxes. Soren's watch didn't look like it was gold, but it had a nice clean face, and it looked like a good watch. One that would last for a long time.

Bo picked it up and held it. It looked small in his hand.

'When we got him ready,' he said, 'when we took him down to the freezer and wrapped him up, I took the watch from his wrist. He wore it so tightly, always. There was a mark on his wrist where he wore it. He never took it off – he was afraid to lose it. It was his father's watch. He always wore it, for all the time I knew him.'

Bo put his cigarette out. He rubbed his forehead.

'I don't know why I took it, but I couldn't leave it. I didn't want it to stop ticking.'

He turned to me and smiled then, a strange smile.

'When I hold the watch in the palm of my hand like this,' and he showed me his open hand, the face of the watch right in the centre, 'I can feel the ticking through my skin – and it's like the heartbeat of a little bird when you hold one, a pulse that you might miss if you are thinking about other things. If you are not concentrating. And I keep thinking, shouldn't a watch be more fragile than a man?'

Bo wiped one of his eyes with the back of his hand and then he wiped his nose too. He looked up at me, blinking – maybe decided now.

'Soren was my good friend,' he said. Then he got up. He said it was no good sitting here in the night, the two of us. He said that if we had some hot chocolate then maybe we would feel like sleep again. When he left the room and went into the kitchen to heat the milk in the little black saucepan that he had bought especially because he said our saucepans were terrible and he couldn't make anything right with them, I carefully picked up the watch from the table. It was warm from being in Bo's hand.

I closed my eyes so I could feel the ticking there against my palm – like the heartbeat of a little bird. But no matter how hard I tried, I couldn't feel it. I couldn't feel the cogs of the watch moving inside.

ONIONS

There was a pile of onion slices on the bench, a pyramid of them – thin and see-through. Bo looked up at me but his hands did not stop moving. He kept slicing onions, running them back and forth quickly against a large metal slicer. He was slicing so fast, the sunlight through the porthole caught the particles of onion juice in the air, and there was a whole rainbow of it there in the galley.

Bo's eyes were puffy and red and my eyes started to water. The acid of the onions was like a wall, invisible but there all the same.

'Go and stand near the sink,' Bo said, still slicing. 'Look down into the hot water.'

The metal sink was half full of steaming water and I leant over it. I could feel the warmth of the steam against the skin on my face. It felt good.

'Stare into the water. Try not to blink.'

I stared down, my eyes wide until the water became blurred and the edges of the sink rounded and then were

gone altogether. Then there was just a body of water – my eyes staring down into a moving body of water.

I blinked. The onion sting was gone. I stood up, my nose running.

Bo was on the last onion. He finished quickly, then slid the pile of sliced onions into a huge metal pot. It was blackened and dented on the outside, but shiny bright on the inside. He wiped the bench down, wiped down the slicer, and then stood over the sink of water. He blinked his eyes. Huge tears squeezed out and they ran down his cheeks but he did not wipe them away.

'I don't like to make French onion soup,' he said. 'So many onions! It tastes so sweet, but it comes from pain!'

I had never had French onion soup. I didn't know what it was. I didn't like the sound of it, but when Bo's eyes were clear and he had washed his hands and set the big pot on the gas ring, he added a whole packet of butter and the smell of the onions gently sweating in the butter made me change my mind about the soup.

There was garlic, lots of crushed garlic, and then more butter. Stock from another pot, clear and brown, that Bo ladled in, and then red wine, a big spoonful of flour. A pile of herbs, like little trees tied together with string, and then Bo stirred. He stirred until the mixture bubbled and then he put the lid on.

The smell was sweet and sour, warm butter and salt and onions.

Bo washed his hands again, wiped them on a tea towel. He stood opposite me, hands down on the bench.

'When I was just a mess boy, maybe seventeen, on my first ship, I had to do lots of the prep in the galley. Cutting onions was one job I always had. I always hated this job! My eyes used to really weep. I could hardly even keep them open. There were no portholes to open in the galley, because it was low down, somewhere under the waterline – by five or six onions I could not see. I would have to keep stopping. I would take so long to just cut the onions. I would get yelled at every time.

'One day, one of the cooks told me that if I wanted to cure myself of onion sting, all I had to do was rub onion in my eyes hard for about thirty seconds. He told me, "You will cry and cry but after, you will never cry again!"

'The cook who told me this didn't mean to be nasty – in fact he was a nice man. He never imagined I would be stupid enough to do it. He felt so bad. I think he almost cried when he saw me. When we got to Gothenburg, in Sweden, two days later, he took me to a bar and bought me lots of drinks. Anyway, my eyes swelled up and closed so that I could not open them at all. I was like this for hours. The first officer told me I was an idiot. He washed my eyes out with water and gave me strong painkillers that put me to sleep.

'I was very young. I never had any reason to doubt what people told me. That was how I grew up – on my island you knew most of the people nearby and they knew you

and you trusted what they said. I knew that I would have to toughen up a bit after that, get a bit smarter. I learnt a good lesson.'

I looked up at him, at Bo – his eyes watching the past, somewhere distant. Somewhere I could not go.

'I always believed what people told me,' Bo said again. 'It feels like a long time ago now.'

Bo opened a cupboard and the top shelf was full of Danish coffee, stacked in rows. Shiny red and silver foil like Christmas decorations.

'Time for coffee,' he said.

I knew he would make me a cup of tea, and he'd say, 'Tea? I don't understand tea.' But he'd make it for me anyway and put in milk and sugar. He would have thick black coffee in his cup which was stained and cracked and always had a teaspoon in it.

'Shall we sit here or go to the mess?' he asked.

We stayed in the galley. I liked it there. The portholes were large and square and let in all the light, and the red booth was soft and lived in.

Bo opened an orange packet of biscuits and they were round and golden. I dunked one in my tea.

'I keep these for when the expeditioners are sick,' Bo said. 'If they are sea sick, I make them eat two biscuits. They tell me they can't eat anything. They say, "Please. No!" their eyes rolling around in their head.'

Bo smiled then, takes a biscuit.

'When we leave Hobart they are all excited, in party mode. A few hours later, they are all outside "calling someone".'

I drank my tea. I didn't know what that meant exactly, but I knew it would be worth it. On *Nella*, I'd never feel bored or lonely or tired. There would just be moments of ocean and sky and ice, merging and flowing and passing by, and when I looked out the porthole I'd know that I didn't have to be anything other than how I was.

MS *Nella Dan*
Voyage 3, 1986/1987 Season
28th January 1987
Position: 60° 54.000' S, 99° 12.000' E
Captain's note: We've been able to find some light winds and calm seas, a rare occurrence on this voyage to date. We crossed the 60 degree south mark overnight and today we have our first negative air temperatures, letting us all know we are definitely in Antarctic waters.

We work hard.

Roast beef, roast pork, three whole poached salmons. Red cabbage, and onions and golden potatoes. Beetroot salad, cucumber salad, cakes and pastries – the special rice pudding with berries and almonds. Brandy hot chocolate topped off with cream.

The lights go out. A flaming magnum of akvavit to end the feast.

The captain stands, he welcomes everyone. He welcomes us all. He starts his speech.

'The King of the Southern Ocean has cast an eye

upon us, and has declared that we are of sound but watery character. So we may pass!'

Expeditioners start to clap, but he continues.

'Today we cross the Antarctic line and become true and trusted friends of this good and special place, the south. May we take good care of it for now and always. I raise a glass to King Neptune – *Australis Rex* – and to our good ship, *Nella Dan*.'

A cheer goes up, a cheer that fills the mess. I hear the words, yelled out with heart – *Nella Dan! Nella Dan! Nella Dan!*

But now, I am standing on the trawl deck – watching the swell lines roll up higher than mountains behind us. Two light-mantled sooty albatross glide off the stern, effortlessly. I can't take my eyes from them.

Somewhere below, the crew are singing 'Home by the Sea', crammed into the Frozen Inn. I will join them soon, when I have taken it in. I will join them when I have had my fill of the wonder of this place.

The Southern Ocean.

WONDERS OF
THE UNIVERSE

A man walked into the classroom and stood in the middle of the room. He had brown floppy hair and bright blue eyes and he looked very awake when he moved – alive and alert. Ready. He was wearing a white lab coat.

'My name is Mr Wilkins,' he said.

Then he turned around, walked out of the door. 'Come on,' he yelled.

We stayed sitting at our desks looking at each other. We were strangers. It was the first day of high school and I had been put in Unwin house. No one else that I knew from primary school had been put in Unwin. It was just luck, which house you got into. Luck, or family connections.

My brother would be put in the same house, Unwin. He was stuck with the decisions that had been made for me.

Slowly a few of the boys stood up and moved to the door. Someone said, 'Is that our teacher?' but no one answered.

We followed Mr Wilkins out of the building and down the hill to an undercover quadrangle. He was standing in the middle of the concrete floor, hands in his pockets.

'This is the outdoor gym,' he said, 'at least that is what I call it. Sometimes there are assemblies here but not very often. However, we will be here often.'

We stood in a huddle together, unsure of where we should stand or what we should be doing. Mr Wilkins pulled a yellow rubber ball from his pocket and bounced it hard against the ground. He caught it in his hand and bounced it again.

'Who knows how to play Four Square?'

A few kids raised their hands. I didn't. I didn't know how to play.

'Right!' he said. 'Rules are simple. I'm your home-room teacher. You can come to me with any problems – anything. We will meet every morning for ten minutes before your first class at the start of the day and then once a week on Fridays for home room – one hour.'

Mr Wilkins walked over and tapped a boy with curly hair and glasses on the head. 'Name?' he said, and the boy said, 'Nicholas Perkins.'

He handed the ball to Nicholas Perkins. 'You are king.'

Then he tapped me on the head. 'Name?' he said, and I told him. 'You are queen.'

He kept going, tapping people on the heads. 'Jack . . . dunce . . . dungeon. Dungeon. Dungeon. Everyone who is not in one of the squares is in the dungeon. The king serves

by bouncing the ball in his own square and onto another. When someone misses a shot – let's say the queen,' and he looked at me, 'then everyone moves up one square and the queen is chucked off the throne and goes to the dungeon at the very back of the line. Got it?'

Mr Wilkins grabbed my shoulders and moved me into one of the squares, the queen square. The other kids formed a line in the dungeon. I wanted to raise my hand and tell him that I still didn't know how to play, but Mr Wilkins threw the ball at Nicholas and yelled, 'BEGIN!'

The game had started.

After a few nervous minutes we were all going with it. I was in the dungeon after two goes, but it came back around so fast and then you were out of the dungeon and playing again in no time. Mr Wilkins made us call out our names when we got out of the dungeon. And it made us laugh – the speed of it. We seemed to be yelling out our names over and over. I guess this was his way of learning our names, but by the time the bell rang, almost deafening us in the concrete gym, we had learnt each other's names too. We had become a group, a home room. A class that seemed to have a lot of kids who were good at maths and science and I was one of them and that was okay. We had Mr Wilkins. He was our home-room teacher.

We were lucky.

We walked back to our classroom, sweaty and panting, and I saw kids I recognised from primary school looking down at us from their second-floor windows. They were

stuck in their home rooms, in Ransom and Hodgkin and Mather – houses that would beat us at every single sporting competition for the whole of my time at high school. And Mr Wilkins said, 'Right! You all have me for physics now, so get your books and lab coats and follow me up the stairs to the incredibly amazing physics lab, where the mysteries of the universe will be unravelled!'

I suddenly felt very hopeful about school and about everything.

MRS HADLEY'S
TYPING ROOM

Most mornings, even when the sun woke earlier and earlier each day, there would be frost on the windows of our car, and on all the cars in the whole of West Hobart. It was my job to wash the thick slabs of opaque ice off the glass with cold water. You couldn't use hot water, or even warm water. The sudden change in temperature could crack the windscreen. I had never seen this but I was frightened of it happening every single day.

Sometimes, the ice was stubborn and would stick fast to all the windows of the car and I would have to use my hands, rub at the ice while pouring the cold water from the watering-can. My hands would stay cold all day at school. Cold right down to the bone.

It was because of the cold that we would all run into the assembly hall as soon as the doors were opened by one of

the head teachers. The yell of 'No running!' wouldn't stop anyone.

There were three wall heaters on the back wall and standing near them was the only way to get through assembly without your legs freezing – without your hands freezing. In the hall you could see your breath, even in the summer.

Year 7 kids never got near the heaters. We were pushed away by the older kids. Still we ran anyway – still we tried.

We all had to sit on the ground, on the wooden floor. There were no chairs. I think it was part of the Quaker thing. Hardship. The moment of silence was a Quaker thing too, and it seemed to go for a long time. Just my thoughts. My thoughts and the cold. How long a minute can be. The long loneliness of a minute.

There was hardly any relief from the cold at school. The buildings were all so old, with thick stone walls. Dark corridors ran down into the depths, deep down into the cold earth. But there was one room that was warm. Mrs Hadley kept the small wooden typing room *toasty* with an electric fan heater.

'Cold fingers are no use for typing.'

Everyone loved typing, but we only had it once a week.

JJJ space FFF space JFJ space FJF space.

The rhythm of tapping the keys, the warmth of the room – it was like having a break from the world. The wooden classroom was on the very top floor of one of the oldest

buildings at school. It was one of the old boarding rooms with a pitched roof and ceiling.

I used to imagine young boys sleeping there in small bunks under grey woollen blankets. I only ever imagined the scene in black and white like an old photograph. That didn't take much imagination, because the walls were cream and the carpet was grey. But Mrs Hadley's hair was fire-engine red and she'd chant in her strong Scottish accent, *SSS space LLL space SLS space LSL space.*

MS *Nella Dan*
Voyage 3, 1986/1987 Season
20th March 1987
Position: 67° 2.000' S, 62° 9.000' E
Captain's note: Holding position in Horseshoe Bay – At Anchor.
Icebergs with the occasional growler. Pack ice.

The last of the ingoing Mawson wintering team was transferred ashore this morning. We will leave for Hobart at 18.00.

A man stands on the deck in the low light as we pull away from Mawson. I cannot see his face. I cannot know what he is thinking. He stares out at the place that has been his home, all he has known for more than a year. Months of darkness and months of light. He watches it all get further and further away – the ice cliffs and the mountains behind the base, the landscape of frozen earth, of rocks, of white, of silence – knowing that he will never return. Knowing he will never see it again.

Soft snow begins to fall, one of the rarest things to happen here in this desert. I go inside. I leave him be.

WORLD OF HIS OWN

I watched Bo out there through the glass door. He was in a world of his own. And all around him were tiny sparrows. They got so close, like he was one of them. Like they were not afraid of him.

One bird was young, its feathers all fluff, and I saw how he made sure it got some bread too. No matter how much the bigger birds pushed it and bullied it, he made sure it got some. It even took a piece of bread right from his fingertips, and it stayed by him as it ate. It stayed near.

He turned and saw me then. I opened the door carefully, tried not to disturb the birds, but they flew off as soon as I stepped onto the deck.

'I keep thinking about my rowboat,' he said. He still had bread in his hand, and he was tearing off little chunks, rolling them tight between his thumb and forefinger.

'It's sitting on the beach with the winter there. I have been away a long time.'

He put the rolled-up pieces of bread in a line on the

railing, but he kept one piece in the middle of his palm – his hand resting, flat and still.

I stood next to him, carefully, not touching. We stayed silent and eventually the sparrows came back, even the baby one.

'They have been watching us,' Bo said, very quietly.

The brown sparrows feasted on the rail, their bodies always moving, their eyes looking for danger. They ate all the bread and flew away as quickly as they had come. But one stayed. One stayed on the rail. It had seen the bread on Bo's palm. It walked up and back, up and back, its little head turning, twitching. It got closer and closer and finally walked right onto Bo's hand.

It stood there for the briefest moment, looked at us, then it took the bread up in its beak and flew away.

'The brave one, he gets the prize,' Bo said. He rubbed his hands together.

The sun was shining but the sky was open and clear, the sun so far away.

'I will go home to my island,' he said. 'I will check on my house, maybe paint my rowboat. Then I will come back with *Nella*. It's not very long.'

We went inside and I thought about his island, where the houses were made of wood and not stone, and you could ride your bike from town to town along the coast, the sea always there. The Baltic. And you would never get tired riding because there were only a few small hills. Not like here.

'It's not long,' he said again. 'I will come back.'

GOING HOME

There is this song called 'Going Home' by Mark Knopfler. It's from the movie *Local Hero*.

It starts off slow. You can hardly hear it, just acoustic guitar gently plucking out the melody, some soft kind of sounds in the background, like the sea and the wind and the open sky all there inside the song. Calling. It's haunting and wanting and saying goodbye.

Then it builds up, becomes electric, and the guitar echoes metallic – still soft, still slow, but when the drums start the song becomes hopeful – joyous, like a victory march.

Look at all that's happened. Look at all that's changed.

We sat in the car in Kingston, parked on the side of the road on a bend, and watched *Nella Dan* sail away.

I got out and walked to the edge as far as I could. Below me was a steep drop, a cliff – rocks and trees and then the water. Mum turned the stereo right up and the music moved like mist in the air across the water – reaching out to the little red ship.

I hoped Bo knew we were here, that we were watching, saying goodbye. I thought I should wave in case he could see us, but that was stupid because he wouldn't be able to. He would be in the galley, already working. He would be inside, busy.

Mum had made him a tape and maybe he had it on. Maybe they were playing it in the galley. Maybe he was listening to the same song.

I knew he really liked it.

The first time he heard it in the car he said, 'I know this song. Yes.'

He told us that he went to see Dire Straits in Copenhagen before he came here, and they ended the concert with 'Going Home'.

'Great song,' he said. '*Nella Dan*'s song.'

The song finished and *Nella* was a long way out, the Derwent no longer a river but the sea. And when I looked at her, she looked so happy heading out to open water. Going home. Going home and leaving us behind.

There were rafts of birds sitting on the water out there, shearwaters – brown-black masses of them, and when I turned back to the car, Mum was crying.

I waited for a while before I opened the door. My brother asked if we could go and get breakfast at a café. It was something we never did, something we had never done.

I don't know where he would have got the idea from. My brother could still surprise me sometimes.

But it made Mum smile.

'Okay,' she said. 'We'll go to a café.'

We drove to a place in Sandy Bay, right near the beach. They had so many things on the menu, but mostly they had lots of different types of pancakes. Pancakes with blueberries, pancakes with bacon and eggs, pancakes with baked banana and maple syrup.

My brother's serve had so much whipped cream on top that he had to dig a tunnel through the cream to get to the pancakes. He was full after about ten mouthfuls, and he seemed genuinely sad to leave so much behind. He'd tried his best but the pancakes had won.

We both knew that we would probably never go to that café again.

It would take six weeks for Bo to get home. He would have one month off, then go to his house, be on his island and walk along his beach. He would check his rowboat and he would paint it, orange and blue.

He would take it out on the water, go fishing. He would fall asleep in the sun on the long summer days when the light was always there. And why would he ever want to come back here?

THE PROPERTIES
OF MATTER

Mr Wilkins liked to use the blackboard. There was a brand-new whiteboard next to it on the long front wall of the science lab. It was much larger and cleaner, but Mr Wilkins always used the blackboard.

He could write so fast in chalk, faster than any teacher I had ever seen. He was determined. It was a dance – his arm moving and his hair moving, chalk dust flying. Sometimes the piece of chalk would snap in half with his intensity, but he'd just keep on going like he hadn't noticed the chalk break.

When the piece got too small, he would chuck it behind him, not with any malice or force, just with enough energy to throw it over his head and get it to land where we were sitting. We would try to catch the chalk without getting off our stools, and if we did he would say, 'Good catch,' without turning around, his arm still moving, his body blocking most of what he was writing.

A few words here and there at the edges.

Particles

An electric circuit

Ohm's Law

Testable hypothesis

Then he would finish, the piece of chalk motionless between his thumb and finger. He would stand and read what he had written, then slowly step aside.

The great unveiling.

Sometimes there were equations. Sometimes a lesson plan or a grand new topic like *The Laws of Thermodynamics!* Sometimes it was a story or a poem, something that seemed not to relate to physics at all. Once it was even a joke. *Why is 'Osmium' the greatest name for a heavy metal band? Because it is the heaviest and hardest metal on the periodic table.*

No other teacher seemed to use the blackboard, so Mr Wilkins' words would often stay there for days. I would look at them in other classes. In biology and in chemistry. I would look at them and wonder if anyone else had noticed, if anyone else had read them or thought about them.

There was one that stayed for weeks, maybe even a month. It stayed and it haunted me and I don't know why. But it hurt to read the words, to think about them and to see them, and yet I wanted them to be true and I wanted to know how to make them true. I looked at them every day until they were finally gone, finally wiped away.

In blue chalk, written in capital letters that took up the whole blackboard. Just a few sentences, screaming:

EVERYTHING IS ENERGY AND THAT'S ALL
THERE IS TO IT. MATCH THE FREQUENCY OF
THE REALITY YOU WANT AND YOU CANNOT
HELP BUT GET THAT REALITY.
 IT CAN BE NO OTHER WAY.
 THIS IS NOT PHILOSOPHY.
 THIS IS PHYSICS.

Albert Einstein

WOODEN SPOON

Bo had asked me what I liked at school and I said woodwork and physics. That was all I liked.

'At least you like two things,' he'd said.

Woodwork. I chose woodwork as my art elective. There was the drama-art-music stream or the woodwork-technical drawing stream. I was the only girl in woodwork. It meant Mum had to buy me another lab coat, a grey one. They were expensive because they were made of a thick material for protection. Protection from flying chisels and burning hot lathe tools. We had big clear eye goggles too, but we could borrow them.

I liked woodwork because it was something I could do. It was something I could understand and I didn't feel so lost in that class. I could think about my grandpa and the things he had taught me about wood. About making things. I could think about watching him in his workshop down

in the garage under their flat and how I used to help him by handing him tools one at a time. He made me a doll's house when I was small. It even had a little toilet that he carved and the lid went up and down and everything. It was made out of scraps of wood, so they were all different colours, different types of wood – but he painted the whole thing and that brought it to life and then it looked like a real house. A big colourful family house. Every room was a different colour and the kitchen was bright yellow.

Our woodwork teacher was Mr Forrest and he had worked at the school for a very long time. I don't think he really wanted to work there anymore. That's what everyone said. I'm not sure why he stayed, but he seemed not to mind the woodwork class so much.

We started with simple things – *simple box one*. Then *simple box two*. It was to teach us measuring and cutting techniques, joining techniques. 'Measure twice, cut once,' Mr Forrest said, over and over.

'Measure twice!'

Once we passed the box components we could move on to more interesting things. Like a carved wooden salad spoon. First, we had to choose the right wood and then we could make the curve of the spoon any way we wanted – as rounded or straight as we liked.

'Flat spoons are strong but boring, curved spoons are more interesting but can break. Find a medium.'

He told us to just draw freehand on the wood and then cut, to just feel the shape.

'Don't think about it,' he said.

I hesitated for ages, holding the pencil tight between my thumb and finger. I kept trying not to think about how a wooden spoon should look. I was frozen. Finally, when the tip of my soft pencil touched the wood, I just drew. I just made a shape, fluid like a wave. And it looked good, quite curved, but good.

It took a long time to cut and then to carve, especially the spoon bit. But it started to look like a real spoon, one that you might buy at a craft stall at Salamanca Market. The colour of the red gum I had chosen was warm honey and orange, with thin lines of blond, clean and bright, and it smelt like the bush on a hot windy day.

I sanded down all the edges and made it smooth, made it soft. It really had come out well and I was thinking about how Bo would really like it and maybe he could even use it in the galley when he came back. He could use it for soups or for salads, take it with him on *Nella Dan*.

But then Mr Forrest broke it.

There was a bend test. Every spoon was tested by Mr Forrest. The spoons flexed between his hands, one by one, and he snapped mine into two pieces.

'Not strong enough,' he said.

I looked at the two halves of my spoon. I knew he had used great force to break it. I had seen how his hands had strained.

I walked away with half my spoon in each hand and went back to my workbench. I tried very hard not to let

anyone see my face because I had gone really red. Each piece felt solid and good in my hands. I was sure my spoon was good. But it was useless now. Even if I glued the spoon back together it could never be used.

I packed up my bench quickly, swept the floor and collected all the wood shavings in the dustpan, put them in the woodbin. The bell went. I took my lab coat off and rolled it up tightly, put it in my bag. I went to leave, but Mr Forrest asked me to stay behind.

I waited near my bench with my schoolbag and watched everyone else leave. The woodwork lab was at the very bottom of the school, bottom of the hill, and it took ages to get to other classes. I had English next, which was in the old part of the school. Not as far as the science labs, but it would still take a few minutes to get there, even if I rushed.

Mr Forrest eventually came over to where I was standing. He put his hands on the bench, looked down. He told me he was very sorry, that he had not meant to break my spoon and that he couldn't explain what happened.

'It was a good spoon,' he said. 'It was good. Sometimes I . . . it was a mistake.'

It was raining again. Steady. Unstoppable. I'd get saturated on the way to English.

'My washing's been on the line for five days,' he said.

I looked at him, his face tired and worn.

'I just keep waiting for the rain to stop.'

I stood there not knowing what to do. I looked at the clock on the wall and I was already late. I asked if I could go and he said, 'Yes. You can go.'

At the end of the term Mr Forrest gave me an A+ for woodwork. He wrote, 'I hope you will continue on, you have a strong feeling for wood.'

LEBANON

My brother and I were watching TV after school. I had a lot of homework to do – to get done – and it was worrying me like it always did, but I didn't want to start. Not yet. I just wanted some time to not do anything.

My brother turned to me and asked me where Lebanon was. I told him I didn't know.

'A man came to talk to us about peace,' he said. 'He was from Lebanon.'

There were often talks about peace at our school. All I knew about being a Quaker was that there were minutes of silence when we were meant to think about peace, and there was grey. Grey uniforms and grey walls.

I got up off the couch and walked over to the small bookcase that was really just a shelf squeezed in between the chimney and the wall. We had a two-volume edition of the *World Book Encyclopedia*. They were brown and black, maybe they were leather, and WORLD BOOK was written in gold letters down the spine. Mum had won them in a

raffle, which was lucky, because I often needed to use them for homework.

I took down the L–Z volume and carried it back to the couch. I opened it up to the beginning of L.

LEB.

Lebanon is a small independent republic at the eastern end of the Mediterranean Sea. The name of the country comes from the snow-capped Lebanon Mountains. In the Arabic language it is called LUBNAN. Lebanon's capital and largest city is Beirut.

I read it out loud and my brother nodded like he knew, like he was being reminded of something that had just slipped his mind. There was a map of Lebanon – long and thin and by the sea. There were also a few black-and-white pictures. One of a giant cypress tree, and one of some ancient ruins with Roman-like columns standing tall without a roof. There was a photo of a clean-looking city, with lots of cars and people walking in the streets and bright white buildings against the sky. One building had a sign on the rooftop that said RIVOLI in huge curly writing.

The caption read, *Place des Canons, Beirut, 1969.*

On the next page there was another picture of the city, only there were no cars and no people walking and the white buildings were gone or so altered that there was nothing there to recognise. Smoke rose from missing rooftops and

everything was blackened or grey. Everything different. The city had been smashed to pieces.

The caption read, *Beirut 1982: Operation Peace for Galilee.*

My eyes scanned down the page then, down all the columns about all the wars in Lebanon. The Civil War and the War with Israel and the War with the PLO. My brother had stopped looking at the pictures, he stopped looking at the book altogether and rested back against the couch.

'No one wins a war,' he said, and he breathed in heavily. 'That's what the man said, what he had come to tell us. No one wins a war, we just all lose. He showed us some photos of his family and he passed them around and told us they were all gone.'

I closed the book and sat with it heavy on my lap. The TV was still on but we were not watching it. Eventually I got up and walked over to the bookcase. I stood there in the corner with the *World Book* in my hands and the room was very still.

'Is the man going to stay here now?' I asked, and I meant forever. I meant was the man going to stay here in Hobart forever.

My brother just shrugged. His eyes were back on the TV and he wasn't thinking about the man from Lebanon anymore.

Only I was.

The story was inside me now. I knew I would remember the man even though I had never even seen him or heard him speak. I didn't know if he was old or if he was young,

but I would think about him, here, living on this island without any of the people he loved or even knew at all. Here, so far away from home, knowing that he could never return to the place he remembered because it was gone.

HAVE A KIT KAT

Advanced maths – my hardest class.

I tried hard to focus, to take the problems one at a time, but they ran at me and began to blur. I could feel the pressure, the clock ticking. There was never enough time. I wasn't smart enough for advanced maths and I didn't know why I was in the class.

Halfway down the page.

There was a girl sitting behind me. I didn't know her very well but she tapped me on the shoulder. She had something in her hand – a Kit Kat.

'Have a break, have a Kit Kat,' she said.

I didn't know what to say. When I looked over, Mr Anderson was staring absent-mindedly out the window, his fingers entwined in his well-groomed blond beard.

I heard the scrape of a chair. Books slapped down hard on the desk next to mine and the girl sat down in the empty seat. Mr Anderson looked over but he didn't move. He didn't seem to care.

'My name is Charlie,' she said. 'Charly with a y because ie is stupid.'

She opened up the Kit Kat wrapper and the foil caught the sunlight coming through the window. I heard the snap of the Kit Kat fingers and she passed me half, still in the foil.

'Thanks,' I said. I went to say my name but she said, 'I know who you are.'

Her hair was messy, light brown, and her eyes were the colour of a soft sky.

'Ladies?' a voice said. Mr Anderson was standing in front of us. 'Finished already?'

'No,' Charly said, smiling, 'but we have *almost* finished and we need a break. We need sustenance!'

She pronounced the word sustenance slowly, carefully, emphasising the *ance*. It made me smile, almost laugh, but I held it in. I kept my mouth tightly closed. Mr Anderson just stood there.

'Finish and hand in your work by the bell. Keep the noise down.'

'Yes, sir!' Charly said. She started to eat her Kit Kat fingers. I ate mine too.

'Kit Kats are the best,' she said and I nodded. I had never had one before. It tasted good. The milky chocolate and the wafers and the lightness in my mouth.

Charly finished her two fingers and rolled the foil up in a ball.

'Don't you just get sick of it?' she said.

I didn't answer. I wasn't really sure what she meant.

'I just get sick of it. I've got to get out of French. I'm thinking of failing the exam on purpose and then they might let me do typing instead.'

'Typing is good,' I said. 'And woodwork.'

'I wish I was in woodwork,' she said. 'How did you wrangle that?'

'I'm not sure,' I said. 'They just let me.'

'I'm in the science-maths stream – plus French.' She rolled her eyes then. 'I'm just sick of maths, nine hours of science a week, the early starts and all of it. It's all just a big production!'

I had never even thought about it. I had always just finished everything even when it meant I had to stay up until two a.m. trying to keep on top of it all at home.

'Mr Anderson, he's cool. But you know, what if, say, like Mrs Crawford said finish this, and we said no. I mean what's the worst that could happen? What could she do? Yell and scream and jump up and down, and tell us we don't deserve to be here, but she couldn't really do anything. You ever met the principals?'

I had once. They were Quakers, and when you went to their office they made you tea and gave you a biscuit.

'I've been sent there heaps and they always just tell me to try my best and try not to make the teachers mad.'

I liked the way she talked. The way she wasn't scared.

'Sometimes I just get really tired of it,' she said again. And she looked tired like I did, had bags under her eyes

like me. We were only in Year 7, we were only thirteen years old, and we were already tired of it.

I looked at the clock. There was only ten minutes left of class. Charly must have seen me look at the clock.

'I've finished,' she said. 'Copy mine if you want.'

I didn't know how she had finished all the problems so fast. Maybe she was some kind of genius, but I didn't want to slip behind so I did the rest of the problems as fast as I could while Charly sat back, hands behind her head, beaming out revolution.

STONES IN THE SEA

Mr Wilkins told us a story over the forty-five-minute home-room meeting because it was raining and freezing, and even though the open gym was covered by a concrete roof, the rain was coming in sideways at such an angle with the intense wind that it was no good. It was an inside day. It was a day where kids would try to find a place to eat their lunch under some kind of cover, under the awning of the library, or the covered stairwell leading up to the science labs, or the corridors that ran between the buildings.

There were lots of days like that. Antarctic days.

Mr Wilkins said he'd tell us a story about the sea if we liked. So we stayed inside.

'What's the most dangerous thing about being at sea?' he asked.

'Storms!' a girl called Mary said from down the back.

'Wrong!'

'Big waves?' Nicholas Perkins said.

'Wrong!'

Silence.

No one could think of anything, or they were too afraid to say something stupid, like me. My mind was going round and round. I couldn't think, I couldn't look at Mr Wilkins. I kept seeing darkness, cold dark water. I could feel it. I was sinking, heavy in the night, being pulled down. I thought about coming here on the ferry in the dark, how the big waves sounded like they could tear the ship apart. I thought about rounds of oil on the surface of water – slick and shiny, fuel, diesel. I thought about fire. Fire burning on the water. But I didn't say fire, I opened my mouth and said, 'Land.'

Mr Wilkins jumped up from his desk.

'Good girl,' he said. 'The most dangerous thing about being at sea is the land.'

Sounds came from the room, groans, pushed-out breath that said, *How the hell are we meant to know that?*

'Just listen to the story,' Mr Wilkins said.

The wind came in under the door and through the gaps in the old window frames and it felt as if it even came through the old, thin glass itself. The wind came in and blew through our hair and we pulled our grey blazers around ourselves a little tighter as Mr Wilkins sat back on the edge of his desk and talked about leaving the cold of Tasmania behind and sailing his yacht towards the bright sun.

'My girlfriend and I were never going to come back,' he said.

There were tropical islands and the long coast of South America. Coconuts collected from beaches and pierced open

with a screwdriver. There were crabs as big as small tables to eat and juice squeezed from raw sugar cane to drink, and all of it was bathed in sunlight, pure and warm and sparkling – the water calling to them to move on. Keep going. The Caribbean waiting on the other side.

During the long wait at the Panama Canal, their tiny yacht was dwarfed by super tankers, by reefer ships, by the giants of the sea that moved goods around the world. Incredible ships, as big as islands, manned with hundreds of humans working day and night, moving around the earth in nonstop motion, never staying anywhere for long. Moving, moving. The earth spinning on.

Finally, they got their turn at four a.m., and in the dark they began the series of locks. A pilot came on board to steer them, friendly, funny. Two deckhands as well, sleeping on the deck. Then they were through. On the other side. They had left the Pacific and were on the Atlantic. Luminous green water. White sand. It was bliss.

They slowed down, planned to move around the hundreds of islands over as many months as it took. In no hurry, they were where they were meant to be. They were taking it all in.

And on a whim, with the shadowy mass of Cuba just visible when they looked hard at the horizon, Mr Wilkins asked his girlfriend to marry him. It had not been planned. He'd never wanted to marry. It was a stupid thing really. They were fine as they were. They were happy and the sun

shone down on them. But he did it anyway, he grabbed her up in his arms and said *I want to marry you*. And she said *yes*.

They drank a bottle of champagne in the sun, one that had been in the fridge, given to them by a friend when they pulled away from dock and down the Derwent River. All that time ago – a lifetime. A world away.

When the night came they were heading slowly for Cuba. Steady. Mr Wilkins' girlfriend went to sleep but Mr Wilkins stayed up and checked the course every fifteen minutes, knowing they were heading in the right direction, heading straight for where they were meant to be going. The path clear. He set an alarm for every fifteen minutes just in case he fell asleep.

'I woke to a terrible screeching sound,' he said.

There was not even time for them to get their life jackets on, the yacht went down so fast. In twenty seconds, they were in the water. In the water in the dark. Complete darkness with only the stars above their heads. But they could stand. They were standing on a reef, but they could see nothing.

They clung to each other there in the dark, the water swirling and moving around them, and they stayed, not ever speaking, just clinging on to each other and trying to keep their feet touching the rock – the reef, this earth. Just before the sun rose, after the longest night, they saw land just fifty metres ahead. They followed the reef all the way to the small spit of sand. An island, a cay, very small, but land.

Their yacht was only ten metres down under the water, broken in half almost, but there. Mr Wilkins was able to get bottles of water, the first-aid kit and the flares out from inside the punctured cabin, and he and his girlfriend sat on the beach and set off the flares. They sat waiting on the beach, not clinging to each other now.

Knowing it was over.

After the rescue, Mr Wilkins' girlfriend flew to Los Angeles and Mr Wilkins travelled down through South America. They didn't see each other for five months. When they did, it was like they were strangers. When they did, there was nothing there. It was like it had all happened to two other people, like it had been a movie they had watched on a plane. Easily forgotten – lost in time.

The bell rang and I was sitting in an old building at school. Hobart. Tasmania. I could feel the wind and the cold again and it was time to get up and move to my next class. Advanced maths.

'Just a crazy dream,' Mr Wilkins said quietly.

A dream.

HOT DOGS

The house was quiet. The house was dark. I stood in the hallway and listened for the TV.

'Hello?' I said.

My brother was on the couch in the lounge, just sitting there in the dim light.

'What's wrong?' I asked.

He didn't say anything.

I let my heavy school bag fall off my shoulder and it thudded on the ground.

'Is the TV busted?'

He shook his head, then got up off the couch and walked into Mum's room. It was off the lounge, and only big enough to fit her bed. There were no windows, just four stone walls and a small built-in wardrobe.

I watched my brother open the wardrobe door and get out the white wooden box where Mum kept her special collection of fifty-cent pieces. The paint was chipped in places, on the corners and along the sides, and underneath

the paint, the wood was dark and warm and red. Inside, the coins moved across the bottom of the box and clunked into the sides.

'I didn't mean to do it,' my brother said, and he handed me the box. It looked like he might cry, or maybe he had been crying – the way his cheeks were a bit red, a bit puffy.

I opened the latch and lifted the lid. There were nine coins inside. Nine silver fifty-cent coins. There should have been fifty-three. I had counted them many times. I knew the total came to $26.50 but Mum said they would be worth more than that one day. She told me the one dated 1966 was already worth $11 because it was the first year of these kind of coins. But she didn't want to sell it. She was going to hold onto them all until they got to their top value.

I looked at my brother.

'I nearly got hit by a car when I got off the bus,' he said.

I opened my mouth to speak but he kept talking.

'It wasn't today. It was before. I got off and I walked behind the bus and a car came around really fast and hit the edge of my school bag. I ran home but no one was here, and there was no bread or anything to eat and I thought about all the coins because at the shop near the bus stop the hot dogs only cost ninety-five cents.'

He stopped talking then, bit his bottom lip.

Fifty-three coins.

Nine left.

That was twenty-two hot dogs.

I wondered what he did with all the five-cent pieces. They added up to enough for another hot dog.

Twenty-three hot dogs.

'I couldn't stop thinking about them,' he said.

He told me that the woman at the shop thought it was strange that he was suddenly buying hot dogs after school when we never had any money, but she still served him anyway. He said she watched him when he left, out of the window, so he always hid around the corner and ate really fast.

'I don't remember taking so many,' he said.

He blinked his eyes.

'I just get really hungry.'

I couldn't argue with that. I got hungry too.

I looked at the coins in the box and I picked a few up. The 1966 one wasn't there anymore. I shut the lid.

'What are we going to do?' my brother asked.

I didn't know what time Mum was getting home. She was at uni, maybe at the library. Sometimes she didn't get home until late.

'Maybe she won't notice,' I said.

Mum used to look through her change every day for collectable fifty-cent pieces, like the 1986 Commonwealth Games one, or the 1981 Royal Wedding, but she hadn't done that for ages. I went into Mum's room and shoved the box under a pile of sheets and pillowcases at the bottom of the wardrobe.

'We just won't say anything,' I said.

I told my brother that he couldn't have any more hot dogs but I would show him how to make Two-Minute Noodles by using the water boiled in the kettle if he couldn't wait for me to get home. That way he wouldn't have to worry about using the hotplate.

'What if Mum looks in the box?' he said. 'What if she goes away?'

Sometimes Mum would get *fed up* with us, if we'd left the door open so all the heat got out, or if we were arguing about what TV show to watch, or who got to eat the crusts of the white bread when we had toasted sandwiches, because they were the best and went all crispy in the grill. She'd grab her keys, slam the door and drive off. I don't know where she would go, and sometimes she'd be gone for a long time. My brother would ask me over and over if she was coming home.

'Do you think she'll come back?' He couldn't sleep until he heard her keys in the door. Then he'd get up and go out to the sunroom and say sorry – sorry for fighting or sorry for leaving the washing on the line, sorry for whatever it was that we had done wrong.

I'd hear him out there, hear him speak in a small voice, and Mum would say, 'That's okay, love,' and maybe she'd pat his hair and he'd sit by her for a while before she'd tell him to go back to sleep.

I'd stay in my bed and look out at the cold night, and I'd think that we shouldn't have to be sorry for any of it. We should never have to be sorry.

'What if she finds out I spent the coins?'

But Mum never said anything. Maybe she stopped collecting fifty-cent pieces – or maybe she just forgot about the box. The hot dogs became a memory, a story we shared, but chose to forget.

Bornholm
June 1987

My home
No fences
One side the forest, the other — the sea
The deer in the garden
Eat my grandmother's roses
Eat the snow drop berries
Rest down beneath the bushes

I try to get close
To reach out and touch them
But they see me
They run

My home
No fences
The forest and the sea

There is lots to do now, suddenly. To get done.

I hurry to pull the rowboat up onto the beach. It feels heavy on my own in the wet sand and it takes time. The paint is starting to flake away. I will need to sand it back and re-paint, but there is not time now. No time. It will have to wait.

Orange and sky blue. Orange for me, and blue for my father. The colours it has always been.

* * *

I am small. I don't know how old but it's time – the end of summer.

My father and I pull the rowboat up the beach. *He* pulls it. I think that I am helping, my small hands trying to grip on tightly, my feet moving one foot after another in the heavy sand. I can hear my father breathing. He is strong and it is easy for him – but still I can hear how he strains ever so slightly.

We get the boat to its safe place – high away from the water where the tough sharp grass begins. The sand is dry here, loose and soft as dust. I watch my father turn the boat over – its dark slick bottom still good. It will last the winter and we will not have to tar this year.

I am glad. I am better at painting. We paint the boat at the beginning of summer – orange and sky blue. The same two colours it has always been, the colours it will always be.

I paint the stripe at the top orange, my father paints the rest sky blue. 'A fresh coat of paint makes the boat so happy. See how she smiles? Brand-new again.'

We mark the coming of summer and are ready.

'Go and get the oars,' my father says, and I run down to the waterline. I pick up the solid wooden oars, ones that my grandfather made with his hands. His initials are carved in the wood, above where your hands grip on. I run my thumb over the letters: H.J. He was a fisher – a fisherman. I did not know him, but here he is. I carry the oars he made. My grandfather.

I tuck the ends of the oars up under each arm, drag them behind me. I can hear the lines they are digging in the sand, lines that the tide will soon come and erase – my hard work will not leave a mark.

My father has secured the boat. He is waiting.

'What took you so long?' he asks, but he is smiling. It is just a joke. He takes the oars from me and carries both in the air so they don't drag. He carries them with ease, like they are just sticks. We walk together to our house, where the woodstove is on and my grandmother will be cooking something good and warm to eat. Maybe it is roast pork and red cabbage, or maybe it is something else. I do not know, but I am hungry now – the day has slipped away.

Tomorrow my father will join his ship and he will be gone.

I look back at our rowboat, upturned, high and far away from the sea. It will be covered with snow soon enough, the dark sky will sit low then – almost touching the earth – the rowboat waiting alone for the summer to come again. Waiting for the long night to be over.

Copenhagen
July 1987

I sit in a bar, a nice place with candlelight and dark wood and people. The night is coming down outside. Feet walk fast above where I sit, the streetlight there – shopping bags, dinner, home.

'Heart of Gold' comes on the stereo.

A group of young men in the corner sing along, happy drunk. It is *their* song. I drink my beer, my heart beats fast. The harmonica plays, the guitar keeps time, keeps strumming, then the chorus starts up again.

When I close my eyes, I can hear Soren sing along too. Loud, out of tune. Heartfelt.

I smoke a cigarette. I get another beer. The song changes. The night moves. People join me, people continue on their way. But it sticks to me, that song. Neil Young. It comes through in my dreams and I wake humming it, wishing I had never heard it.

It stays with me for the four days we are in Copenhagen.

It goes round and round while I walk. Waiting to leave.
Copenhagen, not Aalborg.

Copenhagen.

It's beautiful here, the streets, and when you look up
you can see all the turrets and towers and spires – gold
and green dragons up high. The past.

Like a dream, I walk the streets. I walk the harbour.
I walk in big circles around this city.

'The meat-packing district,' he said. 'It will be the new
place.'

His town. His dream. Now, just me.

My footsteps echo on these old streets. The cobblestones
slicked with rain, but I don't mind. I keep on walking, to
know that I am here, that I exist.

I keep walking.

Copenhagen.

Nella Dan is waiting.

* * *

You make it home. It's all there is – all that exists.

A bunk – your bunk against the bulkhead. A down duvet,
a pillow. A small desk, a chair, a porthole. A cupboard with
little wooden coathangers inside. A home.

You will be warm, you will be snug. You will sleep like a
baby. You will be tired and sleep – the sound of the engine
loud but constant and warm.

Constant.

When it changes, that sound, you will wake. You will

open your eyes and get up. You will look out of your porthole. You might see ice. You will think, *yes, we have slowed down. We have hit the pack ice*, and the white of the light will be almost blinding. You will blink your eyes, get used to the strangeness of this landscape.

You might watch for a time, mesmerised. You might see a Weddell seal, an Adélie penguin, the black, still water between the ice. You will think, *Okay. Go back to sleep now.* It's two a.m. You need to get up soon. Go back to sleep.

You will lie down on your bunk – your ship steady, vibrating, humming. You will listen to the engines and the hull cutting through the ice. You will never forget that sound. You will remember it for the whole of your life – the *clink click clink*, the scraping, the sharpness.

You will think, *Good ship. Good girl, you can do it.* You will rest your hand against the bulkhead, her body carrying your body. You will feel safe. You will be warm. You will fall asleep listening to the engine thinking, *This is home, the only home I need, and I don't ever want to leave.*

THE LITTLE RED SHIP

They called her the little red ship, but she was big. She was huge.

Buoyed up against the wharf, pushing in against the rubber tyres buffering her from the old wood of the dock. Rainbow patterns of oil on the surface of the dark, dank water.

From here, you could see all of Hobart rise up from the river, the city and the houses going up the steep hills, the mountain there, its face behind the clouds.

We were at the bottom of it all, my mother and my brother and me.

Standing and waving.

For the little red ship had come back, and she was here to stay.

For the summer at least.

SEA MOOSE

Bo told me to sit with Leo in the red booth. Big Leo with his blond beard.

I sat down. There was some kind of fishy smell – strong and thick and rotten. On the table, Leo's open sandwich. Black bread and slimy grey fish with silver skin, glistening and wet. Pickled. Leo took a big bite. Some of the sauce got caught in his moustache. He winked at me, held the bread and fish up close to my face.

'Want to try?' he said, grinning.

I shook my head, tried not to breathe. He wiped his moustache with his hand, ate the rest of his sandwich in two bites. One. Two. Gone.

Bo came over and put my sandwich down, bread with havarti cheese, but the fish smell was still in the air and up my nose, and I could taste it in my mouth. Leo watched me eat.

'We have herring every day,' he said. 'Every day. It makes us strong,' and he flexed his biceps. His arm was like a golden tree trunk.

He picked up a bottle of beer and popped the lid right off on the corner of the table – bang! The lid flew across the galley and landed on the floor.

'Skål,' he said and he lifted his bottle in the air, took a big swig.

I took a bite of my sandwich.

'I make good bread,' Leo said.

It was true. He made good bread. I had never had bread like it. There was always the smell of warm bread on the ship. The smell of bread and something roasting in the oven. The smell of melted butter. The smell of diesel. The smell of hot greased-up engines.

'So,' Leo said. 'School holidays?'

I nodded.

'I used to love holidays. No school forever, it felt like, but then it would be there again. School!' He took another swig of beer.

I nodded again. I didn't want to tell Leo that sometimes the holidays were a bit boring, and there was nothing to do. I never had any money, and sometimes it was a bit lonely. I just walked around a lot.

I looked over at Bo. He was busy making dinner for the crew, preparing a small roast beef. It looked good.

'I spent the whole of school drawing cartoons,' Leo said. 'I got into so much trouble!'

He got something out of his pocket. A small notebook. He pushed it over to me, opened it up and turned it the right way so I could look at it properly.

'Our next T-shirt,' he said.

A cartoon of *Nella Dan* with a trawl net behind, and inside the net was a moose wearing sunglasses, a moose with big antlers. Its face was looking out through a hole in the net, looking very surprised, and underneath it said *MOOSE HUNT 1987.*

I smiled when I saw the drawing. I smiled at Leo, but he looked at me very seriously, his face perfectly still now.

'It's no joke,' he said. 'It is in protection of the rare sea moose. You never know when you might see one.'

He finished off his beer and stood up, a giant man suddenly, his head almost touching the ceiling.

'Well, I'll be seeing you, little moose hunter,' he said, and he winked at me. He took the notebook and put it back in his pocket. He said something to Bo in Danish, then he made a 'Mooooooooooose, mooooooooose' sound, and he walked out of the galley.

Bo put the meat in the oven, wiped his hands on a tea towel.

'They can serve themselves when it's done.'

The ship was mostly empty. Everyone was out seeing friends, eating Chinese, walking, driving, lying in the sun somewhere.

'Let's walk,' Bo said.

We walked. Up through St David's Park and across the outskirts of the city to where the hills began. The quick way, which was the steep, almost vertical route up Molle

Street, where the houses clung on to the sides and looked unnatural and strange, one side taller than the other, the pavement at a forty-five-degree angle to the front door. Old stone houses, leaning out.

'Hills!' Bo said, puffed and breathing hard.

'I hate them,' I said. They burned my legs, made me tired. The wind whipped up and down the streets, wind off the water and cold wind from the mountain.

'But you are lucky,' Bo said, when we were almost at the top. 'Hills are good.'

We stopped walking, caught our breath. Bo looked back at the city.

'From the top you can see everything.'

I looked down. It was a stone city. Old stone, carved out of the earth long ago, and now it felt like a fortress.

Looking at the town from a distance, looking down from the top of West Hobart on the steep narrow streets that I would walk every day, it was like there was no time here. Like the town was frozen – still – the scene almost exactly the same as it would have been a hundred years before.

The houses the same.

The streets marked out the same.

Only the smoke from chimneys moved, rose up.

A dog barked, a car passed by. Small movements – small things almost invisible and silent in the big picture of time. They didn't make a dent.

All else was static – stuck.

It had never been cleared away, what sadness people left behind.

Not by fire or flood.

By earthquake or by demolition.

It was all still here, waiting and heavy.

The old stone city was stuck, and we were all here, trapped inside.

'I like to walk,' Bo said.

MS *Nella Dan*
Voyage 2, 1987/1988 Season
8th October 1987
Position: 56° 52.100' S, 125° 24.100' E
Captain's note: Heading to Davis for personnel changeover
and resupply.

Sun streams through the porthole and the light touches my
face, my skin. I stay there, still for a moment. I close my eyes.

I know it's cold outside, the air like ice. But here in the
galley with this light pouring in, I can imagine that we are
somewhere warm.

I am home on my island, and it is summer.

I've had time to make a cake after lunch. A sponge and
it's cooling on the rack. I will add the jam and whip up the
cream and then maybe go sit out on the trawl deck for a while.

Erik is watching a video in the expeditioners' mess, some
American comedy, and I can hear him laugh every now
and then, really loud. It makes me smile, hearing him like
that. He always watches a video after lunch when everyone
is gone. He says he can't sleep on his break.

'It just makes me more tired to lie there in my bunk listening to Jonas sleep for an hour,' he says. 'And I like films. They make me feel like I'm still part of the world.'

We have a pile of videos and the expeditioners usually put one on after dinner. All sorts, horror, action, James Bond.

Sometimes I watch for a few minutes in the evening, but I can never concentrate. I don't have a mind for TV.

Erik appears in the galley.

'Movie over?' I ask. He shakes his head, nods towards the service counter for the mess. I poke my head through. An expeditioner is standing in there.

'Hi,' I say. 'Did you miss lunch?'

He turns, looks a bit green.

'Sea sick?' I ask.

'No,' he says. 'I'm fine.'

He walks forward, comes over to the counter.

'You're just in time for some cake,' I say.

I pour some cream in a metal bowl and start to whisk. I look over at Erik sitting in the booth, feet up on the table. I tell him to put on some fresh coffee.

'Coffee?' I say. 'Tea?'

'Tea would be great,' the man says. 'My name is Robert. Rob.'

I stop whisking and shake his hand.

'Bo,' I say.

He sits down on one of the stools. He has black hair and brown eyes, looks about thirty.

Erik brings over a cup with the tea bag still in it and a jug of milk.

'Erik was watching a video,' I say. 'Do you mind if he keeps watching?'

'Oh yes – please. Sorry to interrupt.'

Erik grins. 'There's only ten minutes to go.'

I keep whisking. I've always loved to thicken cream like this, with the power of my wrist, with skill and a light hand.

'You're good at that,' Rob says.

I nod and it's done. It's ready.

I spread out some red currant jam and then spoon out the cream on one of the sponge layers. Rob takes out his tea bag and puts it on the saucer.

'Sugar?' I ask but he shakes his head.

I cut into the cake – two slices, two plates. Rob sips his tea. He looks at the slice of cake.

'It's my wife's birthday,' he tells me.

'Oh,' I say.

Rob smiles but it's strained and his eyes are small. He takes a forkful of cake, swallows.

'Do you get to call home much?' he asks.

'No,' I say. 'On the ship it's very expensive and it eats all the wages. The satellite phone.'

He nods, has another sip of tea.

'Sometimes it's worse to call,' he says, and he looks at me. 'I mean with the delay and the short time and everything.'

'Sometimes a letter is a good idea,' I say.

'Yes,' he says. He eats some more cake.

I can hear Erik laugh at the movie. I shake my head and roll my eyes. Rob smiles.

'I thought I'd call for her birthday but she got upset, and it was hard to hear.'

I taste my cake. The jam is not too sweet, just like summer at home. Not too sweet – just right. I wipe my mouth.

'I heard some good advice once, from this old-timer. I think he'd done three winters at Casey. He told me that when you call home, ask them how they are right away. Say, "Tell me about your day. What have you been doing?" Then just listen. You only have a minute or two to call on the satellite and you are somewhere exciting and have lots to tell them – about penguins and blizzards and icebergs – but they are at home and doing all the daily tasks to keep things going. They are sacrificing so that you can be here. So, ask them first.'

Rob looks down at his last bite of cake.

'I will try and remember that,' he says.

'More cake?' I ask, but he puts his hand up.

Erik walks in. 'That was a good movie,' he says.

Rob stands up. 'Thanks for cake,' he says. He looks better, not so green.

'Any time,' I say.

I take the plates and his cup and put them in the dishwasher. I stand there and look out of the porthole. I think about the times my father would call from ports, from Melbourne, from Norway, from Hull. He would tell

me about the albatross and about the whales, about life on the ship and what the crew would get up to.

Amazing stories, and I loved them. But the time would run out and he'd have to go. 'Be good for your grandmother,' he'd say, and the phone would go dead.

I would hold the receiver in my hand, hold it right up against my ear for a long time.

'Papa?' I would say, 'Papa?' because I always had so much to tell him. I always had so much I wanted to say.

There was never enough time.

BY HEART

'I don't like cooking much,' I said.

Bo looked up at me but he said nothing. His hands kept on cutting the carrots and celery in perfect time.

'I'm not very good at it.' I twisted the tea towel in my hands over and over, until it was long and thin and tight.

Bo finished chopping. He stood tall, hands on his hips.

'I started to cook when I was very young,' he said, 'maybe even before school, I don't know. I had my grandmother there to help me. To teach me. My grandmother taught me how to cook.'

I thought about my grandma. My grandparents' second-floor flat was steamy with the salty smell of butter. Sunday lunch. In the small kitchen, my large grandmother stirred the thick soup, and I could hear it bubbling.

Bread dumplings in the metal steam pan ready to be cooked, the dark pieces of crusts chequered the white doughy bodies.

Our job was to set the table. My brother and I would

get the plates and knives and forks and glasses and we'd carefully lay them out on the dining-room table.

It was a green wooden table covered with a lace crocheted tablecloth that came from a country far away, a place I had never been to, but was alive and real in that flat. The walls were lined with tapestries of the old city of Prague. The bridge, the castle and the cobblestone streets. Dark, quiet. Standing forever.

My grandmother's old-fashioned dresses, her beehive hairstyle and her kind, soft accent. She was from a place far away, a place lost in time.

Bread dumplings and svíčková – a thick vegetable soup, sometimes with a cut of meat cooked whole in the soup and sliced later.

The soup was poured over the bread dumplings, and they absorbed it like sponges.

Food for winter.

Food for snow.

Food to put fat on your bones.

'What do you make?' Bo asked.

I put the tea towel down on the bench and got out the *Women's Weekly Cookbook* from the cupboard. I picked through the pages.

'I can make this one.' I showed him *Savoury Mince.* 'And this one.' *Russian Potato Salad with Egg.*

He took the book from my hands, studied the pages

– the pictures. His face was blank but slowly he began to smile.

'Seems like you don't like feta,' he said.

There were notes written in pen next to the recipes that I had made so that Mum could get the right ingredients. Under the Greek salad I had crossed out feta and written *NO!* in capital letters.

'Greek salad is very interesting with no feta!' Bo said.

He turned the page. *Winter Casserole.* I had crossed this one out altogether. I had gone over it with pen in lines and lines so that you couldn't read the ingredients or anything or even see the picture. I had blacked it out.

* * *

'Try and eat some, love,' Mum said.

Big fat chunks of beef sat on my plate – glistening with fat, chunks of carrot, chunks of potato. Mum's casserole. I ate the potato and then I made myself eat the carrot.

I put a piece of beef on my fork and ran it round and round the rim of my plate to get the gravy off so I could see the fat. Three times round, rings of orange-brown gravy like a racing track around my plate. I held the piece of beef up in the air. I could smell it.

I looked up and Mum was staring at me with that vacant look.

'Please,' she said.

I closed my eyes and put the piece of beef in my mouth, tried to chew, but I gagged and the beef came out of my

mouth still pretty much in a solid cube. My brother looked at me. He hadn't eaten anything at all.

Mum was standing on the other side of the bench, her hands by her sides.

'Try,' she said again, softly.

But then the door opened and Dad was home. He put his briefcase down and took his jacket off and then he came and sat down next to us at the bench. Mum got his plate out of the oven, full of brown casserole — it looked a little bit dry. He looked at it but he didn't pick up his fork or knife, he just picked it up and hurled it across the room. The plate flew past my mum's head. Some of the casserole spun off onto the floor, but most of it splattered on the cream wall and the plate smashed into a million tiny pieces. Bits of beef and carrot and potato slid on the wall and slopped down.

'I'm sick of this,' Dad said as he got up and put his jacket on, picked up his briefcase and slammed the front door behind him.

Mum started to cry and my brother and I sat there until the food was really cold, the beef congealed in the brown sauce, and we kept on sitting there until one of our dogs came over and started to lick the floor. Mum said, 'No, no, sweetie,' and got the dustpan and a cloth from under the sink and started to clean up the shards of white plate and the globs of brown gravy.

* * *

'I think this needs to go in the rubbish tip,' Bo said, and dropped the book in the white swing-top bin. My eyes must have opened wide, because then he said, 'Well, we won't tell anyone we did that. It will just be lost.'

He put his hands on his cheeks, pulled a face.

'Oh, where could it be? Where could that wonderful cookbook with such exciting food be? We are lost without it!'

I looked at the bin. I was worried about how I was going to manage to cook without the recipes.

'Food comes from here,' Bo said, and he put his hand on his chest. 'Good food you know how to cook from . . .' and he looked up to the ceiling, maybe searching for the words in English. 'By heart,' he said.

He picked up a pen and the message notepad that was next to the phone and handed it to me.

'You write. My English, not brilliant for writing,' he said. Then he said, 'Your mum is doing her best. I know that.'

I looked down at the pad. I drew small circles on the paper, all in a line. I heard the words he said.

'What about meatballs with pasta? Or a simple omelette with cheese and spinach and bacon. Pan-fried chicken with herbs. That's easy.'

My brother came in and wanted to add hot dogs to the list. Bo laughed at that. He told my brother that it was *very* important to know how to make Danish hot dogs.

'You never know when you will be needing them!' he said.

Bo also put the ingredients for pancakes on the list.

That afternoon Bo taught me how to make a simple pancake batter, one that was foolproof and good, and I didn't worry at all while I was making it. I didn't worry about how it would turn out or if I'd done it wrong. I just stayed there in the kitchen with Bo, while he finished off his vegetable soup.

He told me that when he is cooking, he is a *happy little bear.*

I made the pancakes and my brother said they were good. Not as good as at the café but good all the same.

MR WILKINS

In the middle of Physics, Mr Wilkins started to cry.

No one spoke or moved. There was just the sound of Bunsen burners, the hot hissing of them as we all sat there in our white lab coats.

I tried not to look at Mr Wilkins, but I was looking at him.

'I'm leaving,' he said quietly. 'I'm going to become a doctor.' He looked down at the floor, his brown hair flopped over his forehead. He wiped his eyes with his hands.

'I'm going back to university in New South Wales and I won't be a teacher anymore.'

When he looked up his face was pale.

The Bunsen burners turned off one by one and then the hissing sound was gone. Then there was no sound, not even one squeak on the lino floor as Mr Wilkins told us about the accident. About how he had seen it all from the overpass. About how he had been the first one there.

He told us that the car had hit the boy so slowly that he

would have been fine, he would have just had a sore head and some bruises, but somehow, by some kind of crazy, sick chance, the front bumper bar nicked the skin on the boy's neck and sliced through his carotid artery.

Mr Wilkins started to cry again then. He just stood there by the blackboard crying with his hands covering his face.

'I didn't know what to do.'

Outside the clouds had rolled in and it felt like night was coming down fast. That's what the light was like – the night coming. I was worried that it would be dark before I got home. That I would be walking in the darkness.

The end-of-day bell rang in the hallway outside and the sound cut through the air. It made me jump. There was some shuffling, movement from down the back. Andrew Olsen stood up and walked to the door. He hesitated for a second, holding the door part way open.

'It's okay,' Mr Wilkins said, but he wasn't looking at Andrew. He was looking down at the floor again.

There was a rush of movement then. Most of the kids who sat up the back grabbed their books and followed Andrew Olsen. They didn't even put their beakers and test tubes and Bunsen burners away. They just walked to the door as fast as they could, heads down, almost running. I could hear their voices outside. It sounded like they were laughing.

Mr Wilkins sat on the edge of his desk. He wasn't so pale now. He told us, the ones who stayed, that he was very sad and that he had been sad for a long time – he hoped by

becoming a doctor he could do some good. For someone. Maybe he could put the past away. Leave it there to rest.

'I can't forget that boy lying on the road,' he said.

I thought about the footage that had been on the news – the flashing lights reflecting off a fallen schoolbag. The emblem of a waratah shining out in the dark.

I never knew that Mr Wilkins was there. That Mr Wilkins had been there trying to stop the bleeding. Trying to keep Tom Balinski's heart pumping.

The boy lying on the road had not been alone.

OUT THE WINDOW

The last time I saw Mr Wilkins was in home room at the end of the week. Some parents had come to say goodbye, mothers mostly, and he flirted with them all, made them laugh and blush. He could get away with that.

'Call me Anthony,' he'd say.

'Oh, Anthony, you will be missed!'

Some of the mothers gave him red wine and chocolates and cards, and he kissed them all on the cheek. The room was full of people for ages. When students started to leave, I got in line to say goodbye. I didn't have anything to give him, not even a card. I don't know why I hadn't thought to make one and I wished that I had.

Mr Wilkins shook my hand, a strong firm handshake.

'It's been a pleasure,' he said. I shook his hand back but I didn't say anything. I didn't tell him what a difference he had made. How much he had helped me find a way, some loose path to follow. I didn't tell him. I just left the room quickly, my cheeks burning.

I walked fast towards the bus stop, but when I got halfway to the school gate I could feel the freezing air on my arms. I wasn't wearing my blazer. I'd left it behind. I ran back to the classroom and everyone had gone except Mr Wilkins. He was sitting on his desk, looking out at something far away – the mountains, the stars, at the galaxies beyond the Milky Way. Like he was already gone, staring out at his future.

I grabbed my blazer. It was lying over the top of a chair. 'Maybe everything happens for a reason,' he said. I turned around and Mr Wilkins was staring at me. He got up off his desk, picked up his bag, his red scarf, put it around his neck.

'I don't know. If you keep doing science, if you keep working hard, then you will be able to go anywhere, do anything. You could work on the moon – at the bottom of the sea – Antarctica – Helsinki – Zanzibar. Anywhere. Anywhere far away from here.'

He walked over to me then, put a solid hand on my shoulder.

'I know you will do it,' he said.

Then he opened the closest window, lifted himself onto the ledge, and without looking back, jumped out onto the concrete path. I watched him walk away from the classroom, away from the old buildings of the school, until he was gone, and there was only the empty window and the cold air blowing in.

SITTING AT THE WHARF

It was just us. Me and Bo.

From where we were, we could see all of Hobart rise up out of the river. The city and the houses going up the hills, and the mountain there – its stone face behind the clouds.

We were at the bottom of it all, sitting on the wharf together. Me, with my legs swinging out above the black water and *Nella Dan* across from us, brilliant in the autumn sun.

She was a good ship. *A good ship.*

And like he could hear the insides of me, Bo said, 'You do not know whether a ship is *good* or not until you have been on board for a time.'

He looked down at the water then, the palms of his hands resting loosely on his legs.

Stillness.

'I have been on some ships that were not so good. Just places to work and to sleep and to get through the time. Saving your pay, waiting to go home. But it turns out that *Nella Dan* is indeed a *very* good ship. I have been lucky.'

I looked at Bo's face, the way he was looking at his ship. Maybe he was thinking about his friend, Soren, or about leaving again tomorrow. Or maybe he was thinking about his island, his home. A place far away that I only knew from stories.

A rowboat painted sky blue and orange, a small house made of wood.

Three giant walnut trees all in a row, and the sound of the Baltic Sea.

'Yes, I am lucky,' he said again. 'And tomorrow we head for Macquarie Island.'

I knew about this place. Bo had told me. A green mountain in the sea, so full of penguins and elephant seals that it is hard to walk for them. They are everywhere, on every bit of flat land you can find. On the beaches and in the grasses and even inside the work sheds of the station.

'I think it is one of my favourite places,' he said. 'Yes. Maybe the only thing wrong with the place is the wind. It is almost always windy and there is nothing you can do. It is just this force that is there. But the penguins and the elephant seals and the birds – well, they do not seem to mind. They are fine. It is their home and they are used to such things. They are used to it.'

A car horn blew, and Mum's white car pulled up, the engine running. Bo got up and waved to Mum. He held out one of his hands to pull me up.

'Maybe you will go there one day,' he said.

I got in the car, in the back seat, and Bo got in the front. I turned around as we drove off. I looked through the back window. *Nella Dan* – her red reflection streaking out on the water, the brightest thing in the whole of Hobart. She lit up this whole grey town. I waved to her.

Mum and Bo were talking in the front and my brother was back at home, probably watching TV. We turned the corner and headed up the hill and soon buildings blocked my view, but I kept looking down towards the water anyway, looking for her as I had done so many times. I could hear her calling – calling out to me.

I made a wish then, a kind of promise, that I would go where she had gone, that I would see what she had seen. That I would remember this.

The next morning, when *Nella* was leaving, I was at school and I wasn't really thinking about her. I didn't know then that her engines would not start, that she was late to leave. That she did not want to go. That all the crew and passengers eventually got off and stood on the wharf with their families and friends while the engineers tried to get her engine going. And later on, after everything, people said that it was so strange, because she was always in such a big hurry to get going. Always so eager to get back to her ocean. But this time, she clung on to the wharf of Hobart and it was like she did not want to go.

But she did go, a few hours late. She headed up the Derwent and down past our lookout at Kingston and then out on her way to where albatross and the petrels came out of the mist to see her again. To show her the way.

MS *Nella Dan*
Voyage 3 1987/88 Season
29th November 1987
Position: 51° 29.800' S, 155° 39.700' E
Captain's note: Some of the marine science equipment has malfunctioned, so we head to Macquarie Island a few days earlier than planned. We will try and resume marine research on the return voyage.

Erik sharpens the knives.

I watch him from the red booth – sharpening wand in one hand, knife in the other. Casually, like the ship isn't rocking. Casually, like he has been doing this for all his days.

Music is blaring from the tape player – Judas Priest. Erik's moving to the music now, to the beat, eyes fixed on the blade.

'Living after Midnight'.

His beard is growing, his hair cut short, skin still tanned from the summer against his clean white apron. Handsome even, some might say.

He puts down the sharpened knife, takes a bite of

bread – his lunch. He chews for a time, then picks up a fresh blade and begins his dance.

Happy with his task. Relaxed.

No longer a boy.

A young steward at home, working on his ship.

A man.

THE NEWSPAPER

On the table in the sunroom, the newspaper was open.

A photo taken from up high, maybe from a helicopter or from the top of a steep hill. *Nella* looked like a toy ship, listing on her side in the shallows below. A painted toy ship built to sail in a pond, in a child's bath. A ship that I could hold in my hand.

I had never seen her look so small.

Nella Dan is floating free as experts decide on her future

BY ANDREW DARBY

Hobart

The *Nella Dan* rode at anchor at Macquarie Island yesterday while a final damage assessment was begun to determine the fate of the crippled Antarctic supply ship.

As a decision whether to salvage or scuttle approached, it was confirmed that the ship's Danish owner believed

saving the ship was financially worthwhile but a salvage expert opposed it.

The oil rig tender *Lady Lorraine* used 40 per cent of its available 7040 brake horsepower to pull the ship of 2186 gross tonnes free of a rocky bottom on an early-morning tide yesterday.

The Antarctic Division's spokesman, Mr Peter Boyer, said the *Nella Dan* was now 500 metres offshore at its usual Macquarie Island anchorage. From that point, the ship was swept aground on 3 December, apparently after its anchor dragged in heavy weather.

A division official, Mr David Lyons, said salvage divers taking their first look beneath the hull yesterday found more holed compartments than they had expected. 'But all of those have now been secured in various ways and the ship is sitting quite comfortably at anchor at the moment,' Mr Lyons said.

Mr Boyer said the divers shot videotape of the damage for analysis on shore by the salvage master and the ship's representatives. The two parties may reach a decision today whether to scuttle the ship in deep water off Macquarie or try towing it to port for repairs, Mr Boyer said.

The division's director, Mr Jim Bleasel, has confirmed that the salvage company at first advised that recovery was unlikely, possibly dangerous, and the ship should be scuttled.

Despite this objection, *Nella Dan*'s owner, J. Lauritzen SA, re-calculated the cost of salvage and restoration.

Mr Boyer said Lauritzen had decided last weekend that it would be worthwhile.

If the *Nella Dan* were to return to service next season for a final year with Australia, Lauritzen could expect to pick up about $2 million in charter fees. In a market short of such vessels, it could also expect to have work with other Antarctic nations in later years.

The options being considered are towing the *Nella Dan* to dry dock in Australia for repair, and towing to the nearest sheltered deep water harbour to rendezvous with a semi-submersible ship which could carry it to a shipyard for repair.

A patriarch of Australian Antarctic work, Dr Phillip Law, has suggested that the *Nella Dan*, which has carried about 7000 Australian expeditioners to Antarctica, should be saved from scuttling to become part of a museum.

Mr Boyer said this might be considered by the owner if *Nella Dan* was first able to return to service. 'It appears that the idea of having *Nella* as a museum piece isn't an option at the moment.'

MV *Icebird*

1987/1988 Season

9th December 1987

Position: 54° 30.000' S, 158° 57.000' E

Captain's note: Detour to pick up the stranded crew and passengers from MS *Nella Dan*.

We stand together on the deck of *Icebird*. We pull away. We are leaving our ship behind.

Klaus is next to me. His arm brushes mine, and I can feel the full weight of him there.

'My father and your father,' he says, 'they worked together for a long time.'

I can see my father sitting out in the sun smoking his pipe, his eyes closed.

'You are like him,' Klaus says. 'Yes. I was sorry to hear about him passing so young.'

'Thanks,' I say. I suddenly remember that the only photo I have of my father is there in my cabin, stuck on the bulkhead next to my bunk. My father standing at the top of the gangway holding me up in his arms. Me, just

two, my hands outstretched trying to catch the colourful streamers that were falling from the sky. *Nella Dan*'s maiden voyage – twenty-six years ago.

I look back at her now and she looks completely fine, like there is nothing wrong. But at the base of her bow there are rocks where there should be water. Rocks that have cut into her.

'He loved that ship,' I say, and maybe it's right that the photo is still there in my cabin, staying with her. He would like that.

Klaus nods. I can see the burning in his eyes. He has spent the past thirteen years with her and he knows her better than most.

'It's been a pleasure working with you,' I say. I shake his hand. We pull out further into deep water. *Icebird* feels so foreign and strange and none of us want to go inside. We stay out on the trawl deck together and the air freezes our face and our hands, we stay for our captain and bosun, we stay for our ship.

Someone yells, 'See you soon, *Nella*.'

'Home by Christmas.'

I look up at that gigantic mountain reaching for the sky, Macquarie Island. One of the most amazing places I have ever seen. *Nella Dan* is just a red dot now at the bottom of it all, her body half in the calm water, her body half on the land.

Giant petrels circle over her, looking down.

Goodbye.

I say goodbye.

MS *Nella Dan*
1986/1987 Season
26th August 1986
Position: 42° 53.000' S, 147° 19.000' E
Captain's note: Arrival in Hobart for commencement of
1986/1987 season. We are two full days ahead of schedule.

The light is coming – just early light. *Nella Dan* sails up
the Derwent, our Little Red Ship. The hills are rugged and
wild and rocky, and soon houses cling on along the banks.
It's getting lighter but the sky is grey. The rain comes, but
I stay outside. The rain is soft and I do not mind. I want
to see it all. To take it in.

The smell of trees, not pine but a new smell – a tree I
don't know. Soon a small city grows, a town of hills that
climb up to the face of a stone mountain. A large concrete
bridge ahead.

Hobart.

Many of the crew have friends waiting and know this
place. But not me. This is a new place.

'You will love it,' they say, excited to be back.

The Red Lion, the Dog House, the Hope and Anchor, the Ship Hotel – places I will be taken, live music and dancing and beer on tap. I will be able to walk in a straight line for as long as I want. Pizza and sweet-and-sour pork and not having to cook so much, not having to work so hard. A few days. A welcome rest. Our home away from home.

Nella Dan turns in, slows down. She knows the way, finds her place.

The wharf is old, like ones from home. Wooden and aged, the harbour black and deep and still. The rain comes harder now, but I stay outside on the deck.

Across from me on a small jetty, a child is standing in the rain. The hood of her raincoat is down over her head and it seems like she is sleeping – *early morning, early slumber.* Hidden there, almost invisible in the rain, but I can see her.

I can see.

She looks up suddenly. She looks at *Nella* as if the ship called out to her *Hello! Wake up! I'm here!*

And for no reason at all I wave to her. I wave again and keep on waving and she waves back. A beam of light breaks through the clouds and hits the bow and everything shines red. I take a deep breath of this fresh air and go inside to start the breakfast.

I am filled with hope.

JOY TO THE WORLD

The sunroom was filled with people, Mum's friends and crew from *Nella*, and food filled our round table. My brother had a plate full of cheese and he was walking around eating one slice at a time. He had no bread or crackers, just cheese.

Bo put a record on the stereo and the speakers crackled, that moment of anticipation before the needle found its way to the first song.

An organ, in rhythm. A chord. 'I Heard it Through the Grapevine'.

Mum cheered. It was her favourite, the soundtrack to a movie called *The Big Chill*. It looked like a really stupid movie, but the music was okay. My brother and I had to listen to the album for years and years until we knew every song off by heart. My brother really liked the one about a bullfrog called Jeremiah.

Joy to the World.

Christmas Eve.

There were biscuits and cakes and puddings on the bench in the kitchen, but people were still eating the savoury food on the table. We had to wait. We had to be patient. My brother told me he was going to have a piece of everything all on one plate.

'Even the rice pudding?' I asked.

He squashed his nose up, thinking. 'Maybe not that one,' he said.

He didn't like rice, and he didn't like nuts. There were almonds in the rice pudding. I had watched Bo making it with milk and cream and almonds and sherry and sugar. It smelt like fresh custard. Like vanilla ice-cream.

He'd made some kind of hot red wine for the adults that was full of spices. Cinnamon, nutmeg, Christmas spices. He said that there were twenty-five ingredients in the recipe, but the only one that was important was the bottle of rum.

He'd come back on *Icebird* with the others and they were tired. They were wrecked. They had only the clothes they were wearing and nothing else. Mum went to Target and bought them all underwear and T-shirts and they had to stay at a hotel until they had been interviewed for the Inquiry about the accident. Once that was over they were free.

Now we waited for *Nella* to come back. To see how bad the damage was. To see what would happen.

Bo found my brother and me standing by the piano. He said he had a present for us each and they were waiting in the lounge.

'It's Christmas Eve,' he said. 'This is our Christmas. You have to open at least one present.'

My brother put his plate down on the piano lid. There were still two pieces of cheese left but cheese didn't matter now that there were presents.

We didn't have a tree. The empty and cleaned fireplace was where the presents and Christmas decorations were. A few presents, a few decorations. Silver and red tinsel.

Bo handed my brother a wrapped-up box. Something inside hit the sides when my brother shook the present. It sounded like a jigsaw puzzle. He ripped the paper open. It was a Lego set.

His face busted open into a smile.

'Thanks,' he said. He went to shake Bo's hand.

Bo smiled, shook his hand. 'You're a real little gentleman,' he said.

I held my present. It was rectangular and heavy and I opened it carefully. I undid the clear sticky tape and didn't tear the paper. My brother looked away from his Lego set then.

'What is it?' he asked.

It was a book. An iceberg on the cover, close up with icicles hanging down trying to reach the cold water below. *Antarctic Australia*.

'*Nella*'s in there,' Bo said. 'And *Thala*. All her sisters.'

Full colour pages of ice, of light – of King penguins huddled together on Macquarie Island. And red ships forging through the ice.

'I hope you like it,' he said.

The music stopped. I heard the phone ringing. I had the book in my hands.

Bo walked to the door, to the sunroom.

'They're going to scuttle her,' someone yelled.

'She's on fire!'

Everything was loud then, people shouting, asking questions.

I stood in the corner of the sunroom. I saw Leo in a chair and he had his head in his hands.

'It's not true.'

'It can't be right.'

Someone said, 'Those bastards.'

'She's on fire!'

Fire.

My brother came and stood by me.

'What happened?' he asked. I told him I didn't know.

'Maybe the ship sunk because of the accident,' he said.

I said, 'I guess so.'

'But why is there a fire?'

I didn't know.

Everyone was talking in Danish, and the only words I could understand were fuck and bastards and 5000 metres down.

5000 metres down in the dark.

There were more phone calls. New people arrived and some people left. Our front door stayed open.

Everyone was smoking and the room was thick with it. My eyes burned. Mum told my brother to go to bed and he looked at me.

'What about the cakes?' he asked.

'Maybe tomorrow,' I said.

'I won't be able to sleep,' he said, but he did. He fell asleep quickly.

Mum didn't notice that I was still up. She was hugging her friend Rose, and they were crying. I went outside on the back deck to get away from the smoke. To get away from the feeling of the room.

I stood out there and looked at the sky. It was still light and the night was clear. The stars were coming out, translucent and golden. Planets far away. Mars and Venus and Mercury. The moon was rising, just a tiny crescent. A sliver. I breathed in the air. It was summer.

Bo came out and closed the glass door behind him. He had a can of beer in his hand, the one with the black swan on it. That was his favourite. He didn't drink any, he just held it there.

His face was still and I could not think of one thing to say. We stayed like that, looking up at the sky, listening to the low hum of voices coming from inside.

'Did she sink?' I asked.

He lit a cigarette, exhaled. 'I don't think she was going on her own. They filled her with water. I think it must have taken a long time.'

His voice went strange then he turned away.

She could hold no longer.

I thought about 5000 metres down. Five whole kilometres down from the surface, how dark it would be down there, how cold.

Bo wiped his nose with his sleeve, took a drag of his cigarette and something inside me broke.

His voice came like clouds drifting over the night sky.

'She's not there,' he said. 'Not there. Don't think of her down there.'

She's not there.

THE LAST PARADE

We stood in the silence as a small tug the colour of used-up grease turned in and moved towards the place where *Nella Dan* should be.

Everyone around me had flowers, carnations – red and white, and in the stillness a Danish flag was draped over the wharf. It rested down and touched the black water.

I didn't have a carnation. I had a rose, thick red like blood. It was from our front garden, a late rose – one that should not have been there but was.

A man stood alone at the very end of the wharf and began to play the bagpipes. It was a song I didn't know, but it hit me all the same, the feeling of it. The sound echoed out and went right through me like I was made up of nothing but air.

People from the crowd stepped towards the water, almost one by one, and threw their flowers down – a sea of colour. The pipes stopped playing, but I held onto my rose.

I couldn't let it go.

The tug came closer and the sound of her engines took away the heavy silence. The water pulsed and the flowers bobbed. Some went under, sunk down below the surface and were gone. The crowd pushed forward then. There was noise, shouting. Someone right near me yelled out, 'Shame!', and the sudden jolt of it shook my frame. Others joined in and a growling, 'Boo,' rose up, met the crew of the tug as they docked.

Bo was standing back from the crowd, his eyes down. Maybe they were closed, I don't know, but the booing stopped and when I looked back to the tug, *Nella Dan*'s captain had his arm up in a wave. A firm hand like he was saying, *It's not their fault.*

People were just happy to see him then. People began calling out, 'Hello – hey! Welcome home.'

I saw Benny on the trawl deck, his face tired, his face still, and *Nella* was gone and no amount of yelling would ever bring her back.

I walked up the wharf, away from the crowd.

I let go of the rose and watched it float away on an invisible current.

Red Rose, Red Heart, Red Ship.

EARLY MORNING

I got up early and everyone was still asleep. Everyone except Bo. He was sitting at the table looking out of the big glass windows. The sky was dark purple, just light. A thin slice of time between night and day, and nothing was real yet. Nothing had begun.

Bo was smoking a cigarette. He put it out in the full glass ashtray and smiled at me when I sat down at the table, but his eyes were heavy and grey and I could feel the weight of him there in the room.

I am afraid of the darkness, knowing it will come.

There was room for me there at the table but still I held myself so tightly on the edge of the chair that my legs went numb from the strain and from the cold.

I was always cold, even in the summer. He was leaving in a few hours.

Bo lit another cigarette and for a second it felt like the flame and the glow and the taste of the smoke in my mouth made the room warmer. I felt sleepy, heavy.

'I like your name,' he said. 'Isla is like Island. My home is all islands. We are islands in the water and ships are like home. There isn't a kid who hasn't spent time on ships or ferries or boats, even in the big cities. Being on the water is part of our life.'

I nodded. I wanted to ask him what he was going to do now, if he would go and work on another ship. I wanted to ask if he would ever come back here.

'Things don't always work out like we hope,' he said.

I knew that he was talking about Mum, that there were things in her life that I would never know, never understand. She was her own person – light and dark.

'We will watch the sun rise, you and I,' he said, and as the sky began to turn violet, I nodded and felt brighter. I swung my legs free under the table and there was space. I made a pact there in the silence between us. A pact to stay awake – to be awake and not sleeping when he left so that he wouldn't be alone.

The sun came and lit up the face of West Hobart and Bo spoke so quietly that I could barely hear the words and yet they were there in the room with us.

'I wish that I could stay.'

His words went in. They went in somewhere deep and settled down inside of me, but I did not know then that he meant forever. That he would like to stay and live with us forever.

I did not know that then.

I started to shiver, just slightly and he told me to go and rest in bed for a while.

'I will see you before I go,' he said.

I got up and walked through the door to the lounge. I stood still and watched him like I had done so many times through the glass. His white t-shirt, his rounded shoulders, the way he lent down slightly to one side.

He did not turn around. He did not look back at me, but I knew he could feel me there.

The distance between our worlds so much smaller in that moment.

MIXED LOLLIES

Mum sent me into a chemist in the city to pick up a prescription.

The pharmacist behind the counter was short and he was going bald but only right at the top of his head. He took the prescription out of my hands. I told him it was for my mum.

'It's Joseph,' he said. 'Joseph Balinski,' and he looked at me. 'Your brother was good friends with my son.'

I remembered then. I remembered that Tom Balinski's dad was a pharmacist.

'How is your brother?' he asked.

I told him that my brother was out in the car and I could go and get him if he liked, but that I had to be quick because Mum was double-parked. Joseph clapped his hands together and told me he would love to see him.

'I would love that,' he said.

Outside, Mum had found a proper park just a few metres up the street. I opened the door and told my brother that

Tom's dad was inside and that he wanted to say hello. He didn't move.

'Go on, love,' Mum said.

My brother stared at me. Eventually he got out of the car and walked behind me slowly. I could hear his school shoes dragging on the pavement.

Inside, he blinked his eyes against the bright lights. He was polite. He said hello and Joseph was shaking his hand and saying, 'Wow! Look how tall you are. I can't believe your hair is still so curly.' Joseph was smiling. He was really smiling.

He told us that his family were fine and that his wife was pregnant. Twins.

'It has been so wonderful to see you,' he said to my brother. He told us to come back again soon.

'We would love to see you, my wife and I,' he said. 'We would really love it.'

My brother nodded. He said goodbye.

But out on the street in the grey light I saw his face, hard like stone. He sat in the back of the car and stared out the window, like no time had passed since I had run to the shop with my pocket money to get my brother some lollies because I didn't know what else to do.

HERE STANDS A
PHONE BOX

Lansdowne Crescent and the rain came down now.

I knew every step of that curved road. Every single step. The street was empty like always. A ghost town – a dead town. And even though I could feel the rain and it was wetting my hair and making it stick to my face, I didn't even care about it. But when I got to the phone box, I opened the glass door and went inside anyway, into the stale-smelling cubicle with a concrete floor, with torn phone books, and half-rubbed-off graffiti written in black marker on the walls.

I stood there in the phone box and leant up against the glass. I watched the rain fall. I could feel the cold come up from the ground now that I had stopped walking – now that I was still. I picked up the heavy grey receiver, held it there against my ear. It was working, the phone. I could hear the dial tone purring down the line from somewhere far away.

I thought about Bo. Perhaps on another ship somewhere, travelling up to the east coast of Greenland. Or maybe he was at home sleeping on his little island. A place I didn't have a complete picture of.

Then I thought about that film, *Local Hero*. It's about a man from a big city in the USA who works for an oil company. He is sent to Scotland, somewhere really remote and beautiful, a small fishing village by the sea. It's his job to buy the whole village and turn it into an oil refinery. Everyone wants to sell their land. The people who live there all want to be rich, except one man who lives in a wooden shack right on the sand of the beach. He says he has no need for the money. He says he has all he needs.

The man from the USA spends a long time in this village trying to get this one man who lives on the beach to sell. He tries everything. He spends weeks trying. And somewhere along the way he starts to change. His insides change. He stops shaving and wearing suits. He spends time collecting shells on the beach. He starts to forget about time.

But he gets sent home very suddenly and he doesn't even get time to say a real goodbye. He has to leave in a helicopter and look down at the village and the beaches from above and watch it fall away underneath him.

When he gets back to his modern apartment in the big city, it is night and he looks out at the bright lights of the skyscrapers from his high-rise balcony. He looks out and

he thinks, *Is this my home? This place? I don't remember who the person was who lived here. I don't think I know him.*

There is one last scene in the film – a shot of a phone box. It's the red phone box in the small fishing village in Scotland. It is early morning, I think, fog is coming down and it looks cold. The street is empty. And quiet.

The camera stays on the phone box and the empty street for a long time – in silence. The silence goes on as the camera stays still, zooms in slowly towards the phone box. Then the phone starts to ring. It rings out clean and loud, calling out. And it keeps on ringing. The phone just keeps on ringing, and you want someone to answer it. You want someone to run over and pick up the receiver because you know it is the man from the USA calling. You know he is calling to say, *I am coming home.*

THE PACKAGE

A small package by the door, all brown tape and paper. A package with my name on it, my first name and then the address, Allison Street, West Hobart.

It had a round ink stamp on it, red with two penguins standing side by side and underneath them the words *Macquarie Island.*

I took the package inside, put it on the table in the sunroom. I sat down on a chair and I started to carefully undo the brown tape.

Inside was a letter in an old, used envelope – someone's name had been crossed out in blue pen and mine was written above it. There was something else wrapped in more paper, more tape. Something round.

A roll of film in a black plastic canister.

A roll of film.

Isla,

I am leaving this with the postmaster so it will come with the next ship.

Maybe it will get there when you need it most.

We are fine. The captain lost a tooth and there are some bruises, but mostly we are fine. It was a bad storm, with wind and rain and a swell that whipped up out of nowhere, but we all made it to shore on the LARCs. Everyone did a great job.

Today the ocean is a lake, both sides of the island so calm, asleep. Three days like this – it is so strange! If only we'd been one day late, if we'd stayed out doing the marine survey, if only we'd been delayed in Hobart ...

These thoughts go on and on. What if?

We sleep in the mess, or where we can fit. People here have been so kind and they try to keep our mind off things, hot showers and food, a few good homebrew beers. But it is there always, this bad feeling – *Nella* is there, stuck on the rocks and we can't go out to her, even to get our things. She is just there, but we can't go.

I was sure I could hear her bell in the night, just softly – calling me. Such a sad sound! I don't know if I have ever heard such a thing. Maybe I was dreaming, I don't know, but I went outside because I could not stay there anymore feeling like that.

Outside it was clear, the sun already up – 3 a.m. No wind, almost no sound. Something very strange for this island because there is always wind. Always the sound of the water and the wind blowing in the grass and getting in your ears. I went along the path and I could see *Nella* there, on an angle, stuck on the rocks. I kept walking

towards her, but then I turned away. I could not look at her stuck there, so I went down a path I hadn't been on before.

When you are walking here, you have to be careful. There are elephant seals everywhere and they look like rocks. Then they move or burp and you get a big surprise. Huge fat seals! But there are little ones too, weeners. They have the biggest eyes you have ever seen. Round and deep like space.

I got to a beach and sat down on the black sand. There were giant petrels and skuas looking for food, looking for scraps – baby seals huddled together in groups, sleeping then waking and wanting more milk. Calling out to mum. Still no wind. The ocean dead calm.

Maybe hours went by, I don't know. I wasn't cold. I just watched.

Some little gentoo penguins were about. I could hear them above the noise of the elephant seals. They are shy, nesting in the grass, and it's hard to see them. But then one came out, walked right there in front of me.

I took my glove off so that I could take a photo. I have Soren's camera. It was around my neck when the order was given to abandon ship. It's lucky. I'm glad I have it. I don't want to lose it. My glove fell and landed near the penguin. I held my breath but the gentoo stayed. It didn't run away. Its little orange feet were bright against the sand and it came closer, inspected my glove. It pecked at it a few times, then it stood up and looked right at me. I can't tell

you how long that moment lasted, but everything inside me that was scared disappeared. It was gone.

The photo is probably not straight and maybe it is out of focus, but it shows the moment. How close he was, my little friend who came to say hello. To lift my spirits.

It is for you. A gentoo and my glove there on the sand at Macquarie Island, 6 December 1987.

There are other photos. I don't know if they're good or bad – but they are there and I took them. And then there's *Nella* – our little ship.

Isn't she the best?

A ROLL OF FILM

The photos as they came – black and white.

A rocky beach, huge iced-in cliffs behind. Heard Island.

The sun and the moon in the sky all at once, the soft light always there.

A cape petrel, painted black and white and perfectly small. Bo's favourite bird.

Nella Dan right there on the shore, on the rocks. White letters that spell out *MACQUARIE ISLAND* on round fuel drums beside her – the water calm, the water still. Her body slightly on its side.

Her last days.

The last photo – a gentoo penguin on a dark beach, a glove, and the very edge of a shoe. Bo's shoe.

It is the only picture I have of him – his glove, a gentoo penguin and his shoe. But he is there in the photo, his eyes behind his friend's camera. He is there in the background, taking it all in, silent and still as he was.

I have had these photos for twenty-five years. I have

looked at them so many times that they have become part of my make-up.

A cellular memory. A map. A way.

I hold one up now, black and white. A thin isthmus with triangular peaks reaching for the sky on either side. And behind the photo, the real thing – Macquarie Island, in full colour.

Green where there was none. Green where there had only been blue and grey and white.

'So green,' he said, 'green and like a big wet sponge. You never even knew you missed it, green, until you'd been in the ice for so long. Then it hit you. LIFE!'

This place is special and there is nowhere else like it. She is waiting for you to come, ready when you get here.

The last words sent to me from Bo, written in pencil on scraps of paper, yellow and worn now with time but still the pencil marks are clear.

Your friend,
Bo Anker Johansen

I stand on the bow of my orange ship. Photos are silent but Macquarie Island screams with life.

We had rough swell and strong winds all night, but in the morning at first light – 3.16 a.m. – the ocean went to sleep. Out my porthole, Macca stood tall, dusted with snow as the sun burst open a blue sky.

All the things he told me, all the things he said, were true and real and I am here.

Bo – I am here.

Bornholm

'Papa? Tell me about the sea.'

There is a man.

He is sitting at his kitchen table. Outside it is dark. It has been dark for hours and yet the man has hardly noticed.

It is normal.

It is winter.

It is nothing.

Opposite him sits a small girl – his daughter. It is warm in the kitchen – they are nice and cosy and warm sitting there together eating the dinner that the man has made.

'What should I tell you?' the man says.

'About the ice,' the girl says with a mouth full of fried potato. 'What did you do when you got stuck in the ice?'

The man moves a few pieces of sausage about his plate. He looks at the girl.

'Well, we ran out of apples and we ran out of onions. We worked hard.'

'But did you play football on the ice?' the girl asks.

'Yes, this is true. We played football on the ice. We had a tournament.'

'Did your team win the tournament?'

'I don't remember now,' the man says. 'Mostly it was just for fun – to pass the time. We all fell over on the ice, we laughed a lot.'

The girl nods. She knows this. There are photos of the tournament and she has seen them. Black-and-white photographs. One was taken from inside the ship through a porthole. The men are standing on the bright white ice, a perfect circle of light against the darkness inside.

'And did you help dig her out? The red ship?'

'Yes,' the man says. 'We all did that. We all did some digging. We got her going but it was slow and we were using too much fuel, so we had to stay put and wait. We had to give up on the digging.'

'But who came, Papa? Who came to find you?'

The man smiles. He has finished eating but there is still food on his plate. He puts his fork down, rests his elbow on the table. He leans forward towards the girl – his daughter.

'You know the answers to these questions,' he says.

But the girl shakes her head.

'Tell me, Papa! Because I have forgotten.'

The man leans back on his chair now, his arms by his sides.

'The *Icebird* came but they nearly got stuck too because they did not listen. They never liked to listen to us, so

they had to turn back. That ship could get crushed in an icefloe like an empty tin can – not like us. We were safe. We were in no danger.'

The girl nods. 'Yes, you were safe,' she says. 'And what happened then?'

'The Japanese came in a big icebreaker and they rammed the ice, cracked it like it was just an egg. Crack, crack, crack, and it was all broken up. We were finally free. We were moving again, moving after so long.'

'How big was the ship, Papa?'

'It was very big. It made us look like an ant!'

'And what was the best thing?'

'Well, they gave us some apples. A big bag of apples. I think I have never tasted apples so sweet or good. It is funny how you can miss a thing like an apple.'

'I would not miss them,' the girl says.

'You would miss them,' the man says. 'You would miss them if you did not have them for so long.'

The girl says nothing then. Her plate is empty and she looks at her Papa's plate.

'Do you want some more?' the man asks, but he does not wait for an answer. He picks up his plate, pushes the remaining bits of fried potato and sausage onto the girl's plate.

'Don't tell your mother that I did not eat all of my dinner,' the man says. 'She says I am getting too thin!'

The girl laughs at this and he nods. It is their daily agreement.

'Will I go there?' the girl asks. 'Will I go down to the ice?'

'If that is what you want, then you will go,' the man says. 'You will go anywhere you want to go.'

The girl concentrates on eating for a while. Maybe she is thinking – thinking about the cold water, the colour of it. About the albatross that come out of the thick grey to glide on the wake of passing ships. A kingdom of birds. The water rising higher than mountains.

'Will you come with me, Papa? Will you come to Antarctica?'

There is a man.

He is sitting at his kitchen table. Outside it is dark, but he does not see the darkness now.

The light is coming – just early light. *Nella Dan* is sailing up the Derwent, they will be in Hobart for breakfast and after he will be able to step down onto the solid ground of the small city, a city of hills that climb up and up to the face of a stone mountain.

A family there waiting for him. A family waving. A woman, a small boy with curly hair, and a girl called Isla.

A place he wanted to call home.

'Papa?' the girl says, a piece of fried sausage glistening at the end of her fork.

The man looks at this girl – his daughter. He studies her face for traces of fear, for lines of worry. He looks at the whites of the girl's eyes, at the tightness of her lips.

But there is nothing.

His girl is free.

'I have spent a long time at sea, much of my life. But once you have seen it, you dream about it sometimes, and you know it is there, and that is enough.'

The girl nods. She pops the piece of sausage into her mouth.

Her plate is empty.

'Tomorrow we will pull the rowboat up – it's time,' the man says.

The girl nods again. 'I will help,' she says.

There was a man and he told me about the sea. About the ice and about the light, about the birds that came out from nowhere to talk to him – to keep him company.

It was another world.

At night my bed became a ship on the slate-green water. I would sail under the open sky – the stars pale there, both the moon and the sun shining down at once, and I was not afraid.

It was light.

He gave me a picture of his ship and I put it on my wall with Blu-tack.

It was in black and white, and mostly grey, but I could see the colours there. The red of his ship and the white-blue of the ice. The colour of the sky changing from light to dark and then opening up to blue in patches – moments.

This gentle kindness in my house.

My brother and I walked on the stone streets, the past

there like an owl watching us from the rusty rooftops. Huge eyes and thin sharp claws that tried to pick at us as we walked. Tried to take our warmth – steal our joy – take the light away.

But kindness was a shield.

For a time we walked along untouched, together – a few rays of sun shone down on the crescent that led to our new house. A line of hope.

The little white cottage on the hill. A house that we owned. Red roses against the whitewashed walls. A black heavy door thick and old and solid. A room of my own.

There was a man and he told me about the sea. About the ice and about the light, about a ship called *Nella Dan*. I knew him once, for two long summers – when lots of things happened – and lots of things changed.

His name was Bo.

there like an owl watching us from the rusty rooftops.
Huge eyes and thin sharp claws that tried to pick at us as
we walked. Tried to take our warmth – steal our joy – take
the light away.

But kindness was a shield . . .

ABOUT THE *NELLA DAN*

> 'She was from another time when ships were built to last, and she had a mind of her own.'
>
> Captain Arne Sorensen

There were four 'Dan' Danish ships leased from the J. Lauritzen shipping line – *Thala Dan*, *Magga Dan*, *Kista Dan* and *Nella Dan* – that were used by the Australian government from 1953–1987.

Nella Dan was the most famous of these ships. Commissioned by Lauritzen, with great input from the Australian Antarctic Division, *Nella Dan* was named in honour of Nel Law, the wife of the Australian National Antarctic Research Expedition Director of the time, Dr Phillip Law.

Built by the Aalborg Shipyard Pty Ltd in 1961, *Nella Dan* incorporated all the customary features of her elder sisters: an ice-breaker stern, ice fins and an ice knife. However, Nella had modifications unique to her – a double hull in the engine room and part of the holds, and a dishwasher

were two such innovations. The ascent to the crow's nest was through the interior of the mast, and the ship supplied its own fresh water with an Atlas generator. When she was built, the *Nella Dan* was regarded as setting the standard for polar vessels.

Nella Dan spent twenty-six years in service for the Australian government and she sailed longer and further than any other ship in history in the Antarctic region. She visited every one of Australia's Antarctic stations, and supported major exploratory activities along much of the Eastern Antarctic coastline. From 1981, *Nella Dan* provided a research base for Australia's increasingly sophisticated and prestigious marine science program. On 3 December 1987, she dragged her anchor during fierce winds and ran aground off Macquarie Island. After an intense battle to save her, the controversial decision was made to scuttle the *Nella Dan*.

There has never been another ship that worked for the Australian Antarctic Division that has made those who crewed on her or travelled on her so emotionally attached. She was a special ship – old fashioned, small and comfortable and much-loved. Her crew are remembered as being cheerful and kind, and there was a strong camaraderie on board. For all who worked on her, she was home. Some of the crew were with her for years, a few for over a decade. Six of the Danish crew remained behind on Macquarie Island watching over their ship in 1987. They would not leave her. They are among a handful of people who really

know what happened after she ran aground. But that is their story to tell.

Researching for this book has been a life-changing journey for me. I have made many friends all over the world. I have travelled to Macquarie Island, to Antarctica, to Denmark, and experienced many wonderful things.

I feel very blessed.

I owe it all to *Nella Dan*.

Nella Dan rests at the bottom of the Southern Ocean at 54° 37.5' S, 159° 13.3' E. Twenty-six years of memories, laughter and adventure went down with her. But for those who loved her, she sails on.

'She was the Ship of my Life. She was the perfect ship with the perfect crew – for a young kid just finished school and ready to conquer the world.'

– *Hans Sønderborg*

'I will never forget *Nella Dan*.

She gave me the ice, for the first time, and brought me home from the last.

She opened for me the jewel box of the south in a time now past.

She was a fine ship, with a fine crew and belonged to a braver time.

She is gone now, but her spirit lives on, in hearts, and in memories sublime.'

– *Lex Harris*

'It certainly was an adventure and a privilege to have sailed on and worked with the *Nella Dan* and her wonderful crew. The wooden red coathanger in my wardrobe with the JL emblem in gold always makes me smile.'

— Scott Dempster (Trust me, I'm a Larcie)

'My trip on the *Nella* was one big happy experience. As a "newcomer" on the ship, I felt welcome from the very first day, and during my eight months, I experienced a lot of comradeship. Professionally, I learned a lot, not least from my Chief Steward, Ruben Nielsen.'

— Niels Hanghoej Sørensen

'She was one of a kind. I'm proud to have been sailing with her. And I wouldn't be without those nine and a half months for anything in the world – that was a great time.'

— Jan Riisgaard

'I feel pretty lucky to have been involved with the *Nella* and to have seen the life from both sides as I worked for the Antarctic Division during the 1985 season when we were stuck in the ice. I was asked if I'd like to attend Voyage 1 on behalf of my then boss Dr Simon Wright. I was so excited! I jumped ship to work as a stewardess and was onboard for the 1987 season. *Nella* gets in your heart, it's funny how a ship can do that. I can still remember so clearly the day when we were removed/transported from Macquarie Island by LARC to the *Icebird*. *Nella* was still

on the rocks, listing heavily to one side, and as we passed her there was not a dry eye. The connection between the crew and that ship was mind blowing. Some of the guys had spent a great deal of their lives working and living on *Nella*, and while my time with her was relatively short, I do not think there has been a day of my life where I have not thought about that little red ship.'

— *Trish Richers*

'A legacy for *Nella* should be, that she was the kind host to so many adventures and so many lifelong friendships of expeditioners and crew alike. Thank you for inviting us on board.'

— *Anders Hanghøj Sørensen*

'*Nella* was a great (little) ship, with a great soul. Sometimes I wish I was back there. A once in the life experience.'

— *Allan Kürbis*

'All hands on deck at dawn.'

— *Benny 'the Bosun' Wolle*

'With regards to the loss: while I was not there, I was fortunate to have had eight Antarctic and sub-Antarctic voyages on this sturdy little red ship, so I know how she acted in seas that would sink another vessel. Her will to survive was almost legendary, she was like a mother to us, she would always come to take us home. Wrapped in

the warmth and comforting aromas of food and engine fumes she had a feeling of security and welcome. I too feel the loss of this gallant little red ship *Nella Dan*.'

— *Ivan. G. Hawthorn. Esq. BEM. JP*
International Fellow Explorers Club New York City, New York, USA,
Antarctica 1971 and 1973
Officer in charge 28th and 32nd ANARE to Macquarie Island

'She is still in my mind almost every day.'

— *Per Agergaard Olsen*

'For me, sailing with *Nella Dan* (Northeast Greenland and Antarctica) remains as one of my "life experiences".'

— *Jens Aage Vandenhertz Schulz*

'Know the spirit of *Nella* and her crew will always live on through the good hearts and truth of all who walked her deck.'

— *Coral Ann Rigby*

AUTHOR'S NOTE

Everything in this book is fiction, except for *Nella Dan* – the little red ship. It is true she was beset for seven weeks but it was in the 1985/1986 season and not the 1986/1987 season, as I have fictionalised in this book.

A young sailor, Kim Nielsen, died from head injuries on board *Nella Dan* on 20 October 1985. A very sad day for those on board and for his family. R.I.P.

So many kind people have told me their stories and I have held them carefully in my heart. To all who so generously shared, I hope I have done your ship justice.

I wish with all my heart that *Nella Dan* was still here.

* * *

A number of pieces within this novel have been published as short stories elsewhere.

'No Man is an Island' appeared in *Griffith Review* – Edition 34.

'Across the Bass Strait' was published in *Griffith Review* – Edition 39.

'Lebanon' was published in *Island* – issue 133 (2013) and *Best Australian Stories 2013*.

Thank you to these journals and the editors for acknowledging my work.

* * *

I have used *Papa* for Dad, instead of the Danish *Far*. I am aware that Danes do not use *Papa*, but for reasons I can't explain here, I had to keep *Papa* for my characters. I hope this causes no problems for all my Danish friends. Forgive me!

I was given a grant by the Australia Council to help me survive while writing this book. Thank you!

I also won the Antarctic Arts Fellowship, which allowed me to travel to Casey on *Aurora Australis* – a trip of a lifetime. This book would not exist without that wonderful prize.

Cheers,

FP

ACKNOWLEDGEMENTS

I have had an overwhelming amount of help with this book so there are many people I would like to thank.

Vale Matt Richell – friend, surfer and trusted captain of the Hachette family. I will never forget all you have done for me and your great kindness. I wish that we could have that last beer.

Vanessa Radnidge – amazing friend and publisher extraordinaire, you make everything I write better. Thank you for all of it.

DK – you have put up with me during this obsessive process for many years with grace, a smile and no complaints. Thank you so very much – for the Arctic, for Denmark and for making me coffee. All my love.

Fiona Hazard and the *whole* Hachette Team. I know I found the right home with you.

Finn (Wolle) – you took a chance and met with a stranger. Thank you for sharing the love for your ship and

of sailing the south. I met a good friend that day all those years ago. You and your lovely family took me into your home, fed me incredible food (thank you, Camilla – such a great cook!), and gave me all the beer I could drink. I can't wait to see you all again.

Bo SP – what can I say? Thank you for all the stories, emails, memories, music and generosity of spirit. Truly – I am so grateful. Can't wait to meet you (again). I owe you many beers! 'Comfortably Numb' is for you.

Linda, Amanda, Adam and Apple – the family I found and love.

James, Chiyoko, Haruki and Ikumi – my solid foundations. Thank you for all of the joy and support.

Mum and Steve – for all the chats, memories and great junk shop finds.

Julia Styles – trusted editor and advisor. Always such a great help.

Elizabeth Cowell – for a great edit.

Melisinka, Ivana and Jikara – for all the manifestation, laughter and guidance.

Janey Runci – friend, writer and mentor. You've pushed me more than anyone to write the best that I possibly can. Thank you.

The members of my writing group (past and present) – Helen, Cath, Janey, Liz, Stephen, Sherri, Kim, Ian. Much of this book grew from scraps written at the writing table with you all. Thank you.

Susan Armstrong – my lovely agent, who took me on when there was nothing to gain. Glad to have you on my team.

Mette Jakobsen – thank you so much for all the help with everything Danish – translations, food and Copenhagen travel guide.

Kenn – you took me walking in search of deer (and we succeeded). Thank you for all the research help and memories. Looking forward to seeing you next time (my shout).

Anders – what a great surprise to visit *Lilla Dan*. A day I won't forget. Thank you for all of the help over the years. Catch you soon for another nice lunch.

Kim (Kimbo) *It's Alive!* thanks to you. You have been a great help and cheers for the *Nella Dan* twenty-five-years patches that I took to Casey.

Niels – you answered so many of my questions about being a cook/steward on *Nella* and I thank you for your kindness and patience and excellent emails.

Lindy Jones, friend and bird lover – you found research books for me, sent me postcards and spurred me on. Thank you.

The whole *Orion* team – especially Barry Lyon, Adrian Boyle, Alexander Watson, Susan Halliwell – for your knowledge and passion.

Benny Storm – for your kindness and all the years taking care of *Nella*. Can't wait to come and see you.

Lex Harris – another great friend made on this journey. Thank you for the advice, all of the wonderful photos, the T-shirt and all your stories.

Henrik – cheers for dinner, lunch and a great catch up. Looking forward to hiking in Norway. See you next time.

Ivan Hawthorn – I got lucky the day I met you. Thank you for sharing your decades of knowledge with me. It's been a true honour.

George Wilson – for the footage and stories. I really appreciate you getting in touch.

Tess Egan – for all the great research and library help.

Diana Patterson – for lending me your extensive Antarctic library.

My studio family – Robyn Bunting, Andrew John Delaney, Bin Dixon-Ward, Chris Massey. I will miss you guys.

Kenyan family – Gerald, Mary Vine, Paul, Mary, Joan, Wallace, Hillary, Charles, Julius, Joyce, Ann and Charles – Jambo!

The incredible crew of *Aurora Australis* – Katrina, Peter, Rose, Bob, Rob, Murray, Alex, Doug, Adam, Nick, Wayne, Bec, Tanya, Ben, Joe (Bosun!), Wendy, Evan, Cassie, Matt, Sean, and Master Murray Doyle. You put up with me and my questions and I had the greatest time. Thank you all.

Fellow expeditioners – the best DVL in the world, Leanne (has the key to the chocolate cupboard), Brad, Zach, David, John (Bunker door Red-Heads), Shirley, Lyne (friendly neighbour), Robbie, Pete (top champ), Tom, Febes (dancing to the Black Keys), Chris, Zane, Graeme, Kerryn, Gavin, Tim, Sean, Leon, Paul. I loved travelling with you guys. What a trip we had.

Last, but not least:

Elisa Bryant, Todd Griffiths, Marie Isaacson, Krissy Kneen, Mary Bayley, Kate Stevens, Justin Ractliffe, Louise Sherwin-Stark, Anna Egelstaff, Jon Page, Jacinda Pfeffer, Robert John Watkins, Cathy Campbell, David Rittey, Chris Sims, Nicole Maher, Cameron Stops, Coral Ann Rigby, Alice Wood, Jane Mansfield, Daniel Pilkington, Emanuel Hedanek, Eric Woehler, Niels Glaesner, John Gillies, Trish Richers, Alison Brown, Bob Rowland, Chris Somerville, Chris Currie, Edwina Shaw, Catherine Therese, Phillipa Fioretti, Ben and Marta, Lyne Kelly, Scott Dempster, Mads Solver Pedersen, Angela Volknant, Kate Parkin, Esben Munk Sorensen, Sally Webster, Bob Hamilton, John Jorgensen, Friends of *Nella Dan* (all of you), Greer Hendricks, Kristin Raw and everyone at AAD.

To every single person who talked to me about *Nella Dan*, told me their stories, gave me photos and quotes – thank you from the bottom of my heart.

SUGGESTED PLAYLIST

Pink Floyd – 'Comfortably Numb'

The Beatles – 'Hey Jude'

Cat Stevens – 'Father and Son'

Judas Priest – 'Living after Midnight'

Genesis – 'Home by the Sea'

Dire Straits – 'Money for Nothing'

Fleetwood Mac – 'Go Your Own Way'

The Rolling Stones – 'You Can't Always Get What You Want'

Queen – 'We Are the Champions'

Neil Young – 'Heart of Gold'

Marvin Gaye – 'I Heard it Through the Grapevine'

Three Dog Night – 'Joy to the World'

Mark Knopfler – 'Going Home' (*Nella Dan*'s song)